I0632631

Dating Roulette

D. KELLY

D. Kelly

Dating Roulette
Copyright © 2019 D. Kelly
Cover Art by - Najla Qamber of Qamber Designs and Media
Model Photo by - Lindee Robinson Photography
Models: David and Alyse
Editing by – Lauren Clarke of CREATING ink
Proofreading by – Jenny Sims, Editing 4 Indies
Formatting by – Brenda Wright, Formatting Done Wright

This book is a work of fiction. Any references to historical events, real people, or real places are used fictitiously. Other names, characters, places, and events are products of the author's imagination, and any resemblance to actual events or places or persons living or dead is entirely coincidental.
All rights reserved, including the right to reproduce this book or portions thereof in any form whatsoever. For information contact

Dee Kelly www.dkellyauthor.com

This book contains mature subject matter and is not appropriate for minors. Please note this novel contains profanity, sexual situations, and alcohol consumption and potential triggers.

Dee Kelly
P.O. Box 940123
Simi Valley, CA. 93094
ISBN-13: 978-1-7326394-8-5
ISBN-10: 1-7326394-8-5

Table of Contents

Books by D. Kelly

The Acceptance Series –
Breaking Kate – Book One
Catching Kate – Book 1.5
Releasing Kate- Book Two
Loving Kate – Book Three
Christmas with the Houstons – Book Four

Standalone Novels
Chasing Cassidy
Sharing Rylee
The Evolution of Us
The Last Resort Motel – Room 13
Dating Roulette

The Illusion Series
Just an Illusion – Side A
Just an Illusion – The B Side
Just an Illusion – EP
Just an Illusion – Unplugged
Just an Illusion – Encore

Illusion Series Spinoff Novels
Interlude – Jordan's story
Broken Beats – Darren's story
TBA – Eli's story coming fall 2019

http://www.dkellyauthor.com/all-books

Dedication

To my husband, for being one of the few who reached the coveted eighth date. I wouldn't have it any other way.

Love has nothing to do with what you are expecting
to get - only with what you are expecting to give -
which is everything.
~ Katharine Hepburn

Prologue

Tristan

Ten years ago

"Tristan, why are you so moody today? Did you hear what I said?"

The dreary weather today matches my mood. If only the rain would start falling—then I'd have an excuse to go to class early and get away from Adam. He's starting to ask questions that I can't give him answers to.

"Just tired, I guess. So, let me get this straight— Debbie showed up at your house last night, begged you to take her back, and kissed you, completely out of the blue?" I toss my lunch in the trash. No point in picking at it when I have no appetite.

Adam finishes chewing his chip as he nods his head. "Yup, said she heard I was dating again and realized how much she missed me."

I wonder if anyone will miss me?

"What did you say?"

"After she shoved her tongue down my throat, I told her that I was seeing someone else and I wasn't interested."

Before I get a chance to ask if he told Bexley what happened, we see her storming across the quad. Adam's girl is tiny but mighty. Her dark curly hair cascades down her back and her perky tits bounce as she walks. I'll give it to Adam—he's lucky to be dating her, and since I've been so preoccupied lately, it's nice he has someone to hang out with.

"Hey Bex," Adam stands and reaches for her, but she holds her hand out in front of her chest.

"Don't touch me. Is it true?"

With a furrowed brow, Adam stumbles over his words. "Is . . . is what true?"

She narrows her eyes into slits, and her slow assessment of him even makes me uncomfortable. I've never met a fifteen-year-old girl who can pull off the mom vibe. It's like she can see right through him, but Adam didn't do anything wrong. He just wears guilt like armor.

"I see . . ." Bexley turns her gaze toward me and rolls her eyes before looking back at him. "If you wanted to get back with your ex, you should have just said so. Counting breakfast this morning, we've only been out seven times. The last thing I would have been is heartbroken."

With wide eyes, Adam reaches for her, but she sidesteps him. "Bexley, it's not like that."

"Really? If it isn't like that why didn't you tell me you had your tongue down Debbie's throat last night?"

Adam takes a step back, his eyes glazing over in fury. "I told you I had something to tell you, and you asked if it could wait so you could get some study time in before class."

Bex throws her arms in the air and huffs loudly. "It's always an excuse with you. Whatever. I'm just glad I didn't waste any more time on you. Go back to Debbie. I'm not interested."

Adam gathers his half-eaten lunch and tosses it in the trash. "Yeah? Well, that makes two of us! See you later, Tris." He storms off toward the gym, leaving me with his non-girlfriend.

"Your friend is a real piece of work," she mutters as she watches him disappear through the crowds of fellow lunchers.

"Actually, Adam is a good guy, and Debbie is a crazy bitch who showed up at his house and forced herself on him before he could tell her to get lost . . . which he did as soon as he escaped from her evil clutches."

Bexley laughs, and I swear it radiates down to the pit of my stomach. I've never talked to her one-on-one before, but she's even cuter up close. Too bad she dated Adam because now she's off-limits.

"Evil clutches? That's great."

I shrug but flash her a smile of my own. It feels good to smile for a change. "I wasn't her biggest fan. You were definitely an upgrade. Still could be, if you go talk to him and give him a chance."

"You're Tristan, right?" she asks softly.

"The one and only."

She crinkles her nose, and for some reason, I want to kiss it. "Are you always full of jokes?"

"Not sure about jokes, but I'm good with comebacks most of the time."

Bexley takes me in from head to toe. "You're tall."

"And you're not."

"Jeez, thanks for that."

"Just thought we were pointing out the obvious."

She flashes me a grin. "Well, in that case, you're pretty cute, too."

"Thanks," I reply, and she slugs my shoulder.

"You need to work on your skills, Romeo."

That's not exactly true, but she doesn't know that, so I play along.

"Fine. You remind me of Rapunzel."

Her brows furrow, and the smallest little wrinkle appears between them. It's cute, but I probably shouldn't point it out.

"I'm not blond."

Without a second thought, I reach forward and pull one of her curls through my fingers. "Nope, but you still have awesome hair."

She looks down at her feet and then meets my eyes. "We should be friends. I mean, I should get *something* good out of this dating disaster."

That's the nicest thing anyone has said to me in a long time. Hell, aside from Adam, this is the longest conversation I've had in at least a month.

"You think I'm something good?"

She blushes. "Well, you've made me laugh more in the last five minutes than Adam did during our entire seven dates. I'm not even sure why I kept going out with him. I pretty much knew by the third date it was going to be a disaster."

The bell rings, and I grab my backpack. "How did you know?"

She hikes her bag over her shoulder, and we start walking. I'm following her lead even though she's heading in the opposite direction of my class. I'm going to be late, but I don't really care. It doesn't matter anymore anyway. "When a guy doesn't make you laugh, it's a big indicator you shouldn't be with him. At least that's what my mom says, and she's pretty smart when it comes to relationships."

I don't think I'd want to date someone who didn't make me laugh either. Plus, she might be onto something. In the last five minutes with her, I've smiled more than I have in weeks. "Okay, we can be friends, but we can't date. Bro code and all."

Bexley stops in her tracks and grabs my arm. "First rule of being my friend: learn that a girl can just want to be friends with a guy and not want or expect to date him." She pulls out a pen from her pocket and grabs my hand. "Second rule: I like to talk on the phone. Voices are so much better than texts. See you later, Tris."

She pauses and bites her lip before meeting my gaze. "I know I might seem bossy, but it's just my mood today. I could *really* use a friend. Don't disappear on me, okay?"

Her words are like a punch to the gut. She couldn't possibly know what I've been thinking—no one could.

Swallowing over the newly formed lump in my throat, I nod. "Promise. I could use a friend too."

And that is the absolute truth.

She flashes me the biggest grin and waves before walking away. I stand in the quickly emptying quad until the tardy bell rings. I've never been experienced so many emotions all at once. Not about life and certainly not about a girl. I pull out my phone and enter her number before it comes off my hand in basketball. Adam messed up; Bexley is the kind of girl any guy would want to date.

The sun peeks out from behind the clouds as I head toward the gym. It hits me that I have the opportunity to become friends with one of the coolest chicks I've ever met. No awkward feelings will ever come between us since she's already dated Adam.

Meeting her today was a sign I desperately needed. It's like a guardian angel delivered her straight to me when I needed a friend more than ever. And who knows what could happen? She might even end up becoming one of my best friends all because Adam has a horrible track record with girls. Us being friends might upset him at first, but he'll get over it—he's cool like that. The one thing I know for sure is that Bexley makes me happy, and I haven't been happy in a very long time.

Six years later

"Tris! We did it!" Bexley runs into my arms, and I swing her around in a circle.

"College graduates. Now what do we do with the rest of our lives?"

She slides down my body slowly until her feet find purchase beneath her. The smile she flashes me has been the highlight of my day for the past six years. "You're going to make millions off your video games, and I'm going to become one of the best financial analysts in the country. Until then, we move into our new apartment. You and Adam will carry all the heavy stuff, and I'll delegate where it goes while I get ready for my date."

As I release her from my arms, I take a step back. "You have a date the first night in our new place? What the hell, Bex?"

She lowers her head and looks up at me with puppy-dog eyes. "Don't be mad. We're on date five, and I don't anticipate being out long."

Groaning, I wrap my arm around her shoulder. "What's wrong with him?"

The sheepish look on her face tells me I likely don't want to know. "Don't laugh."

"Oh, this is going to be good."

"Come on, Tris. Please." Bex draws out the please and bats her eyelashes at me.

"I'll try not to. Let me guess . . . he puts ketchup on his eggs?"

She scrunches her face and shudders. "No, that would get him booted on the first date. Everything was great until he picked me up to go swimming at his friend's house. He was wearing socks with sandals."

I release a surprised gasp. "Say it isn't so!"

She crosses her arms and glares at me. "You said you wouldn't laugh." She pouts, and if she were any other girl, I'd kiss her, but she's not. She's my Bex.

"I said I'd *try*. I'm curious though; he committed a cardinal sin in dating roulette. How come he's getting another date?"

"Stop calling it that. I'm dating, not playing a game. I can't help it if I have standards that no man has yet to pass." She bends down and takes off her heels as we walk through the grass to meet our parents. "But to answer your question . . . it was his birthday, and as much as I value honesty, I couldn't break it off."

"Who knows? Maybe it was a one-time thing." I'm always defending these men to her as if I have an allegiance to them, but really, it's the opposite—I just want to see her happy.

"I thought that too, and I even thought I could let it slide as a birthday gift—*against* my better judgment. Then one of his longtime friends showed up late and laughed and joked with him about his awful habit of socks and sandals."

I reach for her wrist and halt our progression. "Bex, I adore you, but don't you think some of the reasons you break up with these guys are pretty superficial? I mean, what are you going to say to this guy? 'Sorry, but last week you wore the wrong footwear, and it's still bugging me?'"

Her lip quivers, and she blinks back tears. "Tris, I can't help who I am. I know what I'm looking for, and I know when it's not there."

"Bexley, you have never once since I've known you been out with the same person on more than seven dates. Usually, it's less than five. I'm a guy; I shouldn't even notice these things."

"You notice because you care about me."

"Exactly, and because I want you to be happy."

"I am happy." Her emphatic reply doesn't fool me.

"I could be mistaken, but I don't think happy people block themselves from emotional connections. You fuck random strangers—which would be fine if you threw a boyfriend into the mix every once in a while, but you don't." I take a deep breath. Fighting with Bex today was not on my to-do list.

"I can't believe you, of all people, are judging me!"

"Are you kidding me? I'm not judging you; I'm worried about you! Me wanting more for you isn't enough — you have to want more for yourself."

Her chocolate eyes meet mine as tears begin streaming down her cheeks. *Shit.* The last thing I wanted to do was make her cry. As I pull her into my embrace, she sobs. "You don't think I want more for myself? Why do you think I do this? I'm not going to settle for just anyone, Tristan. I can't."

As I kiss the top of her head, I murmur, "What are you trying to find?"

She doesn't look up at me, but she squeezes me tighter. "The one. I can't explain it, but I'll know him, and it won't take more than seven dates to find him. He'll be the one who makes me feel butterflies, he'll be the reason I smile, and God, Tris, he'll make me laugh like no one else can. At night, he'll wrap me in his arms and tell me how much I mean to him, and he'll make love to me and fuck me in equal measure. I know it sounds stupid to you, but we give away so many firsts to random people. I want the rest of *my* firsts to be with *him*. I want the man I'll eventually marry to be the only one I ever love. The only one I ever make love to, say I do to, and build a life with."

I pull back and tip her chin until our eyes meet. "You don't sound stupid. If anything, I wish more women were like you—confident, determined, and driven. You'll find him one day, and when you do, it might break my heart to lose my best friend to him, but it'll be worth it to know you're happy."

A brilliant smile lights her face. "That's a date-seven question and the final test."

"What is?"

"Can whoever he is handle you being my best friend. Because, Tris, you're non-negotiable. I'm never losing you— we come as a package deal. And honestly, you need to be adding this caveat to your dating specs too. I'm not letting you ditch me for some girl."

"I'd never ditch you, Bexley." I whisper the words, and she rewards me with a small smile.

She reaches for my hand, and we walk silently toward the spot where my parents and hers are supposed to be meeting us. One day, she'll realize there's a deeper reason she won't let herself connect to her dates. Until then, I'm happy living in the now and watching as she finds the most random flaws in these perfectly normal guys. Bexley is an enigma, but for the time being, she's my enigma.

One

Bexley

Present Day

"What time is your date?" Tristan glances over at me quickly, then looks back at his game.

"He'll be here in about ten minutes. I wish I knew where we were going. 'Dress nicely; it's a surprise,' is all I got out of him." After spritzing on some of my favorite perfume, I join him on the couch.

He shrugs, eyes still on the game. "Maybe he's trying to make it special."

"Probably. I'm just tired of being kept out of the loop by my dates. Everyone wants to take the lead, but no one ever thinks to ask what I might enjoy."

"Sounds like that's an indicator you're picking the wrong men. This is date number three, right?" He tosses his controller down and gives me his full attention. Tris tries hard to suppress a grin, but I can see the twitch in his cheek where his dimple resides.

"You are correct, and considering I'm still dating after all these years, it's obvious I've been picking the wrong men."

With a snicker, he leans back on the couch and raises his arms above his head. His T-shirt rides up, giving me a minimal view of his perfect abs.

Tristan loves being nude. If he didn't have a roommate, he'd be one of those people who sits on the furniture naked. The thought makes me cringe—your private parts shouldn't touch the place where invited guests sit. I've walked in on him in the buff more times than I'd like, which is why I openly admire him now. When I scope him out like a piece of art, it prompts him to put on clothes and keeps me from blushing from head to toe. He's like Michelangelo's *David* but with a much larger penis.

"The third date ... that means tonight is the night where you begin your countdown."

"Not necessarily." He narrows his gaze at my feeble counter.

"Come on, Bex. I'm your best friend, and I know you better than anyone. The first two dates, he learned about you, and you took in all his superficial details. Tonight is when you start judging him."

"I don't judge!"

Tristan snickers. "The lady doth protest too much. You judge, Bex, but I'll give you credit where it's due—you get it out of the way quickly." He brings his fingers to my furrowed brows. "Relax. You're going to need Botox for that eyebrow wrinkle before you're thirty if you don't quit."

"Nice way to prey on my insecurities. Some friend you are."

Tris leans forward and kisses my poorly aging skin. "Any man worth his salt will love your wrinkle *and* you. If only you give him a chance."

"It's not my fault," I mutter, leaning my head on his shoulder.

He pushes back from me, taking away my safe space. "Whose fault is it then?"

I'd love to give him an answer other than the truth, but I can't. Even my two loving parents think I'm just as crazy as my friends do. "Mine . . . but in my defense, my parents set the bar incredibly high. Their love is timeless, their marriage is perfect, and I can't help it if I meet a guy and know sooner than most people would that he isn't going to be the one who can give me that."

Tristan's expression softens. Instead of the teasing smiles, I'm met with adoring eyes. "Are you trying to date, or are you looking for a husband?"

The doorbell rings, and I jump up to get it, but Tristan grabs my hand. "Answer me."

I've never been able to avoid him when he takes that commanding tone. His protective nature is one of my favorite things about him. I bet when he uses that voice in the bedroom, his girlfriends come on command.

I shake my head. I won't let myself think of him like that. "Would it be wrong if I wanted to do both? Date my future husband?"

His baby blues cloud over as an indecipherable expression crosses his face. When he opens his mouth to reply, the doorbell rings again.

"Your third date is here; better not keep him waiting. If he's lucky, he might get to lucky number seven."

"You're a jerk." I'm laughing as I open the door.

"But you still love me."

Bradley's eyes widen at Tristan's declaration, and I flash him a smile I hope seems genuine. "Bradley, this is my best friend and roommate, Tristan. Tristan, meet Bradley."

Tristan already has his controller back in his hands and gives Bradley a classic head nod. "Sup."

"Uh, nice to meet you. Bexley, are you ready? I have a car waiting."

Tristan covers a snort with a cough, and I flash him an icy glare. He decided a long time ago not to play nice with my dates since they're not typically around for long. I often remind him—one day, one of them will stick. At least, I hope that's the case.

"Of course. I've been looking forward to it all day. See you later, Tristan."

His voice softens. "Good night, Bexley. Have a good time."

As I lace my arm through Bradley's, I suppress a sigh. Tristan can be so mercurial. I wish he would have answered my question before Bradley got here. There will be time to ask him about it again later. Right now, I need to focus on Bradley.

Bradley and I met in the lobby of our office building. We were both waiting for the elevator. I was going to my office on the thirteenth floor, and he was going to his on the tenth. Before the end of the ride up, he'd asked for my number. I loved his confidence, and so I gave it to him, and within an hour, he'd called and asked me to dinner. Most guys seem to text, which can be fun, but I'm a voice girl. I love hearing a man speak to me. Especially guys like Tristan who can be funny and sweet but commanding when it's important. As I look Bradley over, I wonder if his confidence comes alive in the bedroom too. Even if it does, the bigger question is—will we make it far enough for me to find out?

Tonight, he wears his blond hair impeccably styled with sexy and stylish glasses. He's a little shorter than the guys I typically go for, coming in at about my height at five feet, five inches. He's wearing a suit like he has on our previous dates. Bradley is a lawyer, and so far, we've been driven in a Town Car for all of our dates. He motions me inside first, and as he steps in, that's when I notice it—his fatal flaw. So much for making it to the bedroom.

I blink, hoping I'm seeing things, but I'm not. *Damn it.* He's wearing loafers and striped socks that match his tie. Not just any loafers either. The kind with the tassels hanging from them. They're expensive, no doubt, but my grandfather wore loafers with tassels. To me, they aren't a manly shoe; they're a grandpa shoe. Then top them off with the striped socks—ugh—that's his second strike, and we haven't even left my house yet.

19

The driver drops us off at a hotel in Hollywood. Warning bells are going off in my head, and Bradley must notice.

"Bexley, relax. I'm not expecting you to sleep with me although I wouldn't be opposed. The bar here makes iconic drinks, and the restaurant has a year-long waitlist. I settled a case for the chef recently, and he offered me a table whenever I wanted one."

I give him a small smile as he helps me from the car. "Dinner I can do. Drinks I can do. Sex is not on the table."

He nods and brings my hand to his lips and kisses it. "Then dinner and drinks, it is." The gesture is sweet, but I swear there's a flicker of disappointment in his eyes. Well, right back at you, Mister Matching Striped Socks and Tasseled Loafers.

We're seated immediately in a quiet corner of the restaurant with two of their specialty drinks. His is something with gin and mine is a fruity concoction that makes me wish I was on a tropical island instead of on this date. That's probably not a good sign.

We both order surf and turf with salads and share a laugh about our identical orders.

"How was your day?" he asks, before nursing his cocktail.

"Busy but good. How was yours?"

"Same. I was back and forth between court and my office at least five times. I should have opened my offices within walking distance to the courthouse, but the building amenities where we are were too good to pass up."

He's right. Our building has a top-notch restaurant, a Starbucks, car wash service, and dry cleaning on-site, and they'll pick up and deliver to your desk for free. The best perk is an on-site concierge office. They'll assist any business or employee in the building with pretty much anything at the push of a button.

I take another sip of my tropical escape before replying. "You must pay a ton in parking with all that back and forth."

Bradley raises what looks to be an expertly waxed brow at me. "My driver is on call twenty-four/seven. My time is much too valuable to be spent driving when I could be working."

I'm trying not to judge him, but he sounds like a pretentious ass. "That's understandable. It's impossible to multitask and drive. One of my favorite things to do on the weekends is take a long drive up the coast. At some point, I'll pull off and get some food and eat it on the beach. Do you ever do anything like that?"

Bradley lifts his glass and motions to the waiter that he'd like another. "Bexley," he says with a smile. "I don't have a license—there's no need for one. I'm constantly working, and when I'm not, I'm attending events, conferences, or socializing. My time is best spent staying focused."

This guy's a total douche, and what pisses me off more is that Tristan is going to love the fact I couldn't even get past the third date—again.

"How do you find time for dating?" I ask as I reach for my glass. If I get buzzed, maybe he won't seem so obnoxious.

He brings his glass to his mouth and eyes me carefully over the top of it as if I'm some skittish kitten and he needs to be careful what he says. In turn, I take a huge gulp of my tropical drink and wish he turned me on as much as the drink does.

"Dating for me, is a casual thing. I'm not looking for love; I'm looking for someone to socialize with and to fulfill my needs if you know what I mean." Bradley licks his lips, and before I can tell him what I think of him, the food arrives. He doesn't even pause before he begins eating, and since I'm starving, I'm content to follow his lead. No point in missing out on an amazing meal.

"No thoughts on what I said?" he asks between bites. At least he doesn't talk with his mouth full—he earns brownie points for that.

"I have plenty of thoughts, but ultimately, it doesn't seem like we're on the same page. You're a great guy, Bradley, a catch by any means, but I'm looking for a husband, and you're looking for arm candy."

His mouth drops slightly, and then he releases a full-bodied laugh. "Brava, Bexley. Perhaps we aren't the love connection I thought we'd be, but you're spunky, and I could use a good friend who will tell it like it is."

"Seriously?"

"Completely. I'm a candid person; life is too short for games and lies. I'm wealthy, Bexley—have been all my life. Grew up in wealth and have developed my own personal fortune on top of it. I don't want, nor need, a wife. I tend to attract a specific kind of woman, and usually, they're the kind looking for a few kids and a huge divorce settlement. I'm a busy man who is happy in his own company. Give me a cigar, an expensive bottle of scotch, and a good book any night over a family."

I'm seeing him through completely clear eyes now. "Wow. Well, at least you know what you want."

He places his napkin to the side of his plate and leans back. "Now tell me the truth: are you truly looking for a husband, or am I just too pompous for you?"

Heat sears my cheeks, the alcohol removing some of my inhibitions. "You're a bit high maintenance for me, but I'm also not into casual dating unless I see a future, and I'm really good at figuring out who isn't a match early on."

"That's fair. Finish your dinner, and I'll take you home. I meant what I said—we will be friends, Bexley. You're exactly what I need in my life."

Somehow, I'm okay with that. I think I can help Bradley loosen up a bit, and he could definitely use it, even if he doesn't know it yet. There's something about him that's endearing, and I'd bet under all his pomp and circumstance, he might be open to falling in love more than he's ready to admit.

Two

Tristan

"Where's Bex?" Adam asks as he plops down on the couch and grabs the second controller.

"Third date."

Adam laughs. "Poor bastard. He has no idea this is the beginning of the end, does he?"

I can't concentrate on this game. "Beer?"

Adam nods, and I grab us both one from the kitchen before sitting back down. "Dude, this game is sick. It's going to make you famous."

"I don't need to be famous. I just need it to work and stop crashing on level five." My frustration gets the best of me as I toss my controller aside. Knowing a whole team of beta testers are working on this game around the clock, I should probably be in the office, but I've been there so much lately, and I needed a break. I thought Bex and I could have a pizza and movie night. I forgot she was in the middle of another round of dating roulette.

"You've got months still before you have to finalize this game."

I open my mouth to give him all the statistics, but he beats me to it.

"I know, one glitch can tank games. One glitch may forever remain unfixable. Breathe, Tris. You're great at this,

24

but you need time to reset. Your mind will work better if it's fresh. When you launched your last game, you said you weren't going to do this to yourself again."

He's right, but it's not easy to disassociate from work when you're the boss. The livelihood of everyone rests on my shoulders.

As I run my fingers through my hair, they get stuck in a knotted curl, which reminds me I'm way past due for a haircut. "I know. Maybe I just need to get laid."

Adam laughs. "Now you're talking. Want to go to the bar?"

"Nah, not tonight. I want to stick around and make sure that sleaze doesn't try anything when he drops Bex off."

Adam eyes me suspiciously and finishes his beer. "So, what is my ex-girlfriend up to these days?"

"Knock it off. She's not your ex; she's not anyone's ex. That's her issue. She hasn't changed as long as we've known her. You're still one of the few reigning date-seven champions, in case you're curious. That takes mad skills. I guarantee you, this guy she's with tonight won't be seeing date number four."

Adam stands and pockets his keys and his phone. "As much as I'd like to stick around to see the loser she's with tonight, I've got an early meeting in the morning. I can't tell you how much I miss the days of raging frat parties and naked beer pong."

"Yeah, no way do I feel sorry for you. I'm sure your job for one of the biggest internet porn providers is extremely taxing."

"It's harder than you'd expect. It's almost wrecked porn for me, if you want the truth. I see more clits and dicks in a day than I ever thought possible."

I shake my head. "Still not feeling sorry for you."

Adam covers his heart and stumbles backward. "You wound me. I'm the better friend in this relationship."

"Agree to disagree on that one."

I reach for the controller I tossed aside, and he thumps the back of my head. "I came over to help with your game and try to cheer you up. You get to play video games all day. Do you have any idea how hard it is to work your way through a marketing meeting with breathy moans and slick skin slapping as your soundtrack? I mean, even if it's not a constant turn-on, sometimes the dick rises to the soundtrack it recognizes. Breathy moans are hard to ignore."

Breathy moans *are* hard to ignore. I hear Bexley when she's getting herself off sometimes, and damn . . . I shouldn't get hard because she's my best friend, but I totally fucking do.

"How do you get around it?" I ask him.

"I've become a master at giving presentations sitting down due to my slipped disc."

I laugh. "You're not even thirty; they actually buy that?"

"My boss is older than shit, and I'm pretty sure he's hiding his hard-on under the same table as the rest of us. The women definitely prefer us sitting so they don't have to avert their gazes. It works for everyone, and I'm not the only one who does it. I just have the best excuse."

I stand and give him a quick bro-hug goodbye. "You're never boring, Adam. Thanks for cheering me up."

"Anytime. Text me tomorrow and tell me when you want to go to the bar. Seriously, you need to get laid. I'll be your wingman."

"Will do."

After locking the door, I decide to take a quick shower. Bex hasn't been gone that long, and I know she's going to ask me about the husband question from earlier. That's one thing about Bexley: she doesn't forget a thing.

Maybe that's why she's so picky with her dates. I'm surprised she manages to ever get laid, but every once in a while, she steps out of her dating cycle and has a one-night stand. It's her preferred method of sex. She says that way there's not much time to find out his bad habits, his sob story, or that he has a total lack of motivation. Unless he's lazy in bed, and then she deems him completely unmotivated anyway.

It's hard to imagine anyone getting the chance to fuck Bex and being lazy about it. As I strip down and turn on the shower, I think about what's been going on with her lately. Ever since we met, Bex has either become easily bored with men or annoyed by their habits. It was kind of funny in high school, almost a game. Even for part of college, because we were still kids, but now . . . we're nearing our thirties, and she's missing out on so much life.

She's never mean when she breaks it off with the guy she's dating. However, she is blunt if they ask why she doesn't want to see them anymore. That's what concerns me the most. Fortunately for Bex, I think the seven-date rule works in her favor. Men don't typically develop an emotional attachment until after they get lucky. We'll work hard for sex, but if the girl hasn't put out by the seventh date, most men will cut their losses.

Bex is one of the best people I know, but I'm worried about her. I don't know any other women with such strange dating processes. What if she looks back as an old cat lady one day and realizes her entire life has passed her by? She swears that won't happen, but so far, the odds haven't been in her favor.

Shaking Bexley from my thoughts, I rush through my shower routine. I dry off quickly before wrapping the towel around my waist and head toward the kitchen. I'm starving. I scope out the fridge and grab another beer. I knew I should have gone grocery shopping today, but Bex and I usually go together. Guess I'm going to order a pizza after all.

Once the pizza is ordered, my game beckons me. I'll only play for a couple of minutes, and then I'll get dressed. That's what I tell myself at least, but when the doorbell rings, pulling me back to reality, I grab my wallet and hope the guy has seen worse than a dude in his towel.

The only problem is when I open the door, it's not a pizza delivery guy. No, I can't be that lucky. It's a pizza delivery girl and not just any girl either.

"Hi! Did you order a . . .?" Her words trail off as she looks up from the sticker on the box. This is the worst time not to be wearing any damn clothes. "Tristan," Kelly says curtly, even if her eyes betray her anger. They rake over every inch of my skin before meeting my eyes. *This is the perfect example of why one-night stands are a bad idea.* "If I'd have known this was your pizza, I would've spit in it."

"Someone sounds angry," Bexley says, walking up the path to our door.

Kelly shoves the pizza at me, and I almost lose my towel. She snatches the money out of my hand, eyes flaring with rage. "Don't think you're getting change. It's the least you owe me. And you." She turns her attention to Bex. "Don't believe anything he says. You don't mean anything to him, and he won't call you the next day or ever again."

Bex raises a subtle brow at me but slides past Kelly before inching up on her tiptoes and kissing me. Her lips are soft and taste like tropical fruit. When I part my lips to taste more of her, she pulls away. *Damn.* The kiss was short but filled with passion that shot down to my toes. We've never kissed like that before, but now I'm wondering why not. "Babe, what am I going to do with you?" Her hand slides seductively down my chest, and my heart skips a beat. I don't know what's gotten into her tonight, but I'm curious to see where she wants to go with it.

"Sorry, Tris was a bit of a brute, but I've tamed him. Thanks for the pizza." Bex moves her hand back to the center of my chest and pushes me until I'm backing up. She closes the door and locks it behind her before bursting into a fit of laughter.

That was hot and wrong all at the same time.

"What in the world has gotten into you, Bexley Marie Scott?"

"I might have had a few cocktails at dinner—strong ones. What kind of pizza did you get?" It's a rhetorical question since she's already peeking inside the box I'm still holding. "Oh, Tris, you got my favorite!"

As she walks toward the kitchen for plates, I put the pizza down and go throw on some sweats and a T-shirt. When I come back, she's comfortable on the couch with her feet tucked under her and a piece of pizza on a plate.

"Didn't he feed you?"

"Calm your rage, He-Man. He fed me an incredible dinner, but you know me. I drank, and now I need a snack. How come you got dressed?"

Her quizzical gaze throws me off. She must be drunk. Why didn't that asshole walk her to the door if she was this buzzed? "Are you a pod person? I'm pretty sure my Bex wouldn't want my junk on our couch, even if it was wrapped in a towel."

"True, I don't, but if I was going to let anyone have their junk on our couch, it would be you."

She tosses a rogue mushroom into her mouth and moans in appreciation. I'm not sure I've seen her like this before, but I like this version of her. Bexley rarely lets herself have enough alcohol to lose all her inhibitions. I'd rather she do it with her friends though, and not with a date she hardly knows.

"I'm going to guess there will be a fourth date. You're in a great mood." I lean back with my plate of pizza and face her.

"Uh, no, date three was the end. He was a good sport, though, and he appreciated my honesty so much he still wants to be friends."

"I'm sorry. What was the final nail in his coffin? Too much styling gel?" I'm not sorry at all, but I do feel bad for her all the same.

She giggles. "He had grandpa tassels, striped socks to match his tie, and he was an entitled prick, but that part I can get past. I think it's a defense."

29

He's not the first guy she's ditched for the tassels. "I swear, Bex, as much as I adore you, having you in my life has given me some serious confidence issues."

She places her plate on the table before responding. "You're the perfect guy, Tris, and you have no clue how much I regret dating Adam because now I can't grow up and marry you one day."

I'm at a serious loss for words, but one thing I know for sure is that she's going to be hungover tomorrow. She's never this candid unless she's had more than her body can handle.

"You also never answered me earlier. Would it be so wrong to want to date my future husband?"

I knew she was going to come back at me with that question, but I never expected it to hurt so much to answer her. "No way, but keep in mind, we're still young. You have years ahead of you to find your husband, and when you do find him, you absolutely should date him. If you're trying to find him in seven dates, I think you need to date him for at least seven years before you get married."

Her chestnut eyes brighten. "That can't happen. I want to have babies before I'm thirty-two."

Babies . . . of course she wants to have babies soon. Bexley hates that she's an only child. I put my plate on the table and tug her into my side. "All your dreams will come true when the time is right. Maybe you need to stop looking and let your husband come to you."

Her eyes flutter closed, and she hums under her breath. "Maybe you're right. All this dating is becoming exhausting. I just don't want to be alone anymore."

"You're never alone. I'm always going to be right here."

She tucks in closer to me and grips my shirt. "Until you find another girlfriend and you get all commanding with her in the bedroom. Damn, that has to be so fucking hot."

I'm biting my lip to hold back my laugh. "Is that something you're into, Bex? Being told what to do?"

"Seems sexy as hell, but I've never done it to know for sure."

Damn it. How much stuff is she missing out on? Her desire to have all these firsts with *the one* I sort of understand. The fact she's convinced she'll know him when she dates him worries the fuck out of me. Bex doesn't see the bigger picture. She could make it to date eight or date eighty-eight, and this guy could still break her heart. It kills me to think of her being crushed like that, but she doesn't seem the least bit concerned. With all the break-ups she's witnessed involving her friends, especially me, you'd think she'd be a bit more cautious.

"Can you promise me something, Bex?"

"Anything . . ." she says on a yawn.

"The next guy you date, give him all seven, no matter what."

"That's a hard promise."

"Please? For me?"

She moans as my fingers weave through her hair. "Okay. For you."

Bexley falls asleep in my arms quickly, and I begin to formulate a plan. Adam gave me permission a long time ago to date her if I wanted to, and I never wanted to risk crossing those boundaries before, but after tonight . . . I'm not sure there's anything I want to do more than date my best friend.

Three

Bexley

My head is pounding, and my breath is god-awful. I vaguely remember Tristan carrying me to bed. When I open my eyes, it's still dark outside, but my bladder doesn't care.

I tiptoe out into the hall and pause as I pass Tristan's room. Even though his light is off, the unmistakable sound of him jacking off carries into the hall. His soft moans and his lube-slicked hand sliding against his cock—I can practically envision it. This is such an invasion of privacy, but our walls are thin. I wish I had the courage to open his door and slide down on top of his slicked skin and ride him until dawn. I wonder if it would be a welcome surprise or if he'd turn me away?

His cries become louder, and I quickly move toward the bathroom. Listening outside his door isn't okay.

After relieving myself and brushing my teeth, I go back to my room and lock the door behind me. Sex is supposed to be good for headaches, so I pull out my vibrator and lube, and take off my clothes.

As I work myself over with my vibe, I imagine what Tris must have looked like while he was getting himself off. I'm picturing his abs tightening as he inched closer to his release. I'll bet his baby blues glazed over with the sweetest kind of ecstasy. And as he came all over his stomach, his eyes would have fluttered closed with pleasure.

My orgasm crashes through me with the sexy images in my mind. *I wonder if he ever thinks of me when he comes.*

The aroma of freshly brewed coffee lulls me from my sleep. Tristan greets me with a smile as I stumble into the kitchen. God love him, he even makes me a cup of coffee just the way I like it.

"How's your head this morning?"

"It's been better," I mumble, as I take the first heavenly sip.

He takes the seat across from me at the table and drinks from his favorite mug. "How much did you drink last night?"

"Too much. Three or four of these amazing fruity cocktails. I couldn't even taste the alcohol, and it hit all at once."

He frowns. "Why didn't that asshole walk you to the door?"

Oh, man. Angry Tris first thing in the morning isn't good. "He wasn't with me. Bradley got called into the office, and he had his driver bring me home. He offered to walk me in, but I told him it wasn't necessary, and it wasn't."

"This time," he mutters angrily.

"Are you mad at me? About last night? I know I said some pretty inappropriate things, and I'm so sorry. The alcohol got to me, and I . . . well, I don't really have an excuse, but I am sorry if I made you uncomfortable."

Tristan's eyes widen, and he practically chokes on his coffee. "I'm not mad at all, and there's nothing you could ever do that would make me uncomfortable. Do you remember your promise to me last night?"

I made him a promise?

"About giving the next guy seven full dates?" he prompts, and it comes back to me. Damn it. I did promise him, and I can't take that back.

"Um, I remember now."

"Good." He smiles and then stands. "I have to get ready for work, but can you and Rita meet Adam and me at Just an Illusion tonight after work?"

I love that bar, and he knows it. "I'll be there, and I'll ask Rita. I don't know what she has planned since it's the weekend and all."

Tristan rinses his cup in the sink and kisses the top of my head on the way out of the kitchen. "Bex, one more thing . . . don't accept any dates from anyone until you and I have a chance to talk tonight. I'll explain why later. Just trust me and promise, okay?"

I draw an *X* over my heart with my fingers. "Cross my heart."

"Thank you."

Rita and I arrive at the bar a little after eight. Tristan called a few minutes ago and said he and Adam are on their way now.

Rita practically bounces with excitement as we walk into the bar. "I'm excited to finally be meeting the elusive Adam."

We slide into a booth, and a waitress greets us immediately. This place always has great service. "Welcome to Just an Illusion. I'm Allie, and I'll be your waitress." She hands us menus, but we don't need to open them. "Can I get you something to start, or would you like a few minutes to look over the menu?"

"I'll have a chocolate martini," Rita says, and that sounds much better than the white wine I was about to order.

"I'll have the same. Our friends will be here in a minute, so can we also get a Hendrick's on the rocks and a Jameson neat?"

"You got it. Would you like any appetizers?"

"Nachos," Rita and I both reply in unison, and Allie laughs.

"They are the best in town. I'll be back with your drinks in a flash."

"Tell me about Adam," Rita says when Allie leaves.

"Well, first of all, back to your original comment—I'd hardly call Adam elusive. You'll probably love him at first sight. He's got red hair like Prince Harry and a slight dusting of freckles across his nose. He was cute when we dated, but he's grown up to be quite a manly man."

Rita eyes me skeptically. "If he's such a catch how, come you haven't given him a second chance?"

The snort escapes before I can stop it. "No one gets a second chance."

"You are the strangest person I know, but I swear if one day you meet the guy who passes all of your tests, I might become a believer and convert."

"It will happen. You just sit back and watch."

Rita's eyes widen as she looks toward the door. "They're here. Oh my God, Bexley, why didn't you tell me he's a walking orgasm?"

"The Prince Harry reference wasn't enough for you?"

"I didn't think you were actually serious!" she hisses before pasting a smile on her face when they approach.

Tristan scoots in next to me, and Rita mouths, *"Thank you,"* to him. He gives her a subtle nod as Adam introduces himself before sliding in next to her.

"Did you get the nachos ordered?" Tristan whispers the question as he leans in close. Goose bumps break out over my arms, and I'm thankful for the dim lighting. Who knew something as mundane as nachos could sound so freaking seductive?

"What do you think they're whispering about?" Rita asks Adam with a flirty smile.

Adam flashes her a salacious grin. "Food. With them, it's always about food."

Tristan shrugs. "Guilty, but the food here is great. You can't really blame us."

"The eye candy is pretty good too," Rita adds shamelessly. Adam subtly inches closer to her. *Let the games begin.*

Allie returns with our drinks and the nachos. "Jameson goes to?"

"Me." Tristan holds out his hand, and by default, she gives the gin to Adam.

"I'll be back to check on you in a bit. If you need something sooner, just flag me down."

"She's so cute." Rita sighs as Allie walks away.

Adam doesn't let the moment pass him by. "So are you. Tell me about yourself, Rita."

The two of them begin chatting animatedly. I'm not even sure they're aware we're still here. It's getting louder in the bar, and tonight's band is warming up, making it harder to hear. Tristan scoots as close as he can get so we can hear each other.

"How long before they ditch us?" he asks with an easy smile.

Rita likes to play somewhat hard to get at first, but that doesn't mean she won't leave and make Adam take her to dinner or something. "Thirty minutes?"

Tristan chuckles. "Adam is halfway through that drink already; I give it fifteen, tops. Did you drive?"

I nod.

"Good. I'll just have this drink, and then I'll be fine to drive us home."

"It's okay; I can stop drinking. I had enough last night anyway. You should have fun tonight."

He looks at me with a heated gaze, but that can't be right. This martini is already getting to me.

"I'd prefer it if you enjoyed yourself. Last night was interesting, and I have some things I'd like to talk to you about. You do better with awkward conversations if you've had at least two drinks."

"But . . ."

He cuts off my protest with that fucking tone that hits me in all the places it shouldn't. "I'll drive, Bex."

"Okay." My acquiescence has nothing to do with me wanting to drink and everything to do with me wanting to know what the hell has gotten into him.

While we eat our nachos, we watch Rita and Adam. I'm a bit envious, if I'm being honest with myself. I've been on tons of dates, more than anyone should probably go on, but I don't think I've ever been that relaxed. It seems so natural with them, and I wonder if it's because eventually, they may end up together or if it's because they're completely comfortable with the potential one-night stand they both know is coming.

Allie comes back, and Tristan orders me another drink and water for us both. Rita and Adam both decline a second drink; they're getting ready to make their move.

Rita kicks me lightly under the table, and I give her a thumbs-up, obscured from Tris and Adam's view. She flashes me a beaming smile before whispering in Adam's ear.

"You two cool if we get out of here?" Adam asks, but he's already standing, and Rita is scooting out of the booth behind him.

I laugh and wave while Tris and Adam say their goodbyes.

My second martini arrives and looks even more decadent than the first.

"How was work today?" Now that Rita and Adam are gone, I somehow feel like we can talk freely.

Tris turns toward me in the booth, which makes it easier for me to see him while we talk. "It was amazing. We figured out the glitch."

"Tristan, that's incredible!" My arms wrap around him instinctively. It's not like we've never shared hugs before, but neither of us moves to pull away. Since we kissed last night, he seems ... flirtier, and I don't mind one single bit.

His mouth ghosts over the shell of my ear, and I suppress the urge to moan. What has gotten into me? This is Tristan, my best friend. "Finish your drink, and let's go home. I have some things I need to discuss with you."

He doesn't have to ask me twice. I down the rest of my martini, hoping that by the time we get home, I'll be feeling the full effects. It's not enough alcohol to get me drunk, but I'll enjoy the buzz as long as possible.

Tristan shakes his head. "You didn't have to pound it, but I applaud your eagerness." He tosses some money onto the table and reaches for my hand to help me up.

Once we're in the car and on our way home, I'm overcome with the sense that after tonight nothing is ever going to be the same between us again.

I just wish I could tell if that was a good thing or a bad thing.

Four

Tristan

The ride home was abnormally quiet. The air between us sparks with anticipation and need. In the past twenty-four hours, I've realized how much Bexley means to me. I've finally admitted to myself that I no longer want to be only her friend. This is ultimately her call, but if it were solely my choice, I'd hop on her dating roulette wheel and never get off.

Once we're inside, she kicks off her heels like she does each night after work. We sit together on the couch, and I pull her feet into my lap. When I start to rub them, she releases a groan that makes my cock ache.

"Can I ask you a strange question?" I ask, while kneading her foot with my fingers.

She moans again, and I reposition her foot so she can't see what effect her noises have on me. "You can ask me anything you'd like as long as you keep massaging my feet."

"Seems like a fair trade." I flash her a smile before hitting her with the question I've been dying to know the answer to. "I've been thinking about you a lot lately—not in a creepy way, I promise. I'm just trying to put all the pieces together about your dating life. We've never really talked about certain things, and I'm curious. If you were saving all your firsts, why did you lose your virginity to some random guy?"

Bexley exhales, and when her eyes meet mine, it's with a weary gaze. "Besides not wanting to be a virgin anymore, which was the main reason, I didn't want to find the man of my dreams and lose him because I was inexperienced. It's stupid, I know, but it's how I felt. How I still feel."

"I wish you would have asked me," I confess without looking away.

"You? W . . . why?"

"Because I love you, and you're my best friend. I would've made sure it was special for you. I hate that something so important to you was done with some random guy, and you ended up doing the walk of shame the next morning."

She pulls her feet away, tucking them beneath her, and props an arm on the back of the couch. After brushing a wayward curl from my forehead, she meets my eyes again. "What is going on in your head tonight? Talk to me, Tris."

"I'm trying."

"Start with telling me why you made me promise not to date without talking to you first."

Reaching forward, I caress her cheek, and she leans into my touch. "Date me next."

I use the tone she calls the commanding one, and her eyes dilate. Fuck . . . it really does turn her on. How did I never notice that?

"Tristan, that's a really bad idea."

"Why?"

"Why? For starters, you're my best friend."

"Exactly." I weave my fingers into her hair, and she moves closer to me. "If it doesn't work, we'll be fine, I promise. I won't let this get in the way of our friendship."

"You say that now but—"

I bring my finger to her lips to silence her. "No buts; we've been through so much already. We can handle seven dates."

"You're assuming you'll make it to the seventh date." As I smile, she gasps. "That's why you made me promise."

I'm about to lay all my cards on the table. "Yes. Bexley, I want my chance to win your heart."

Her eyes close for a long moment, but my hand is still at the base of her neck, my fingers entwined in her curls. "I'm scared, Tris. What if you do something that's a deal breaker?"

"That's always a possibility, but if I do it in the first six dates, you have to let it go. If I do it on the seventh, well, that's a risk I'm willing to take, I suppose. Either way, nothing is going to come between us. *Nothing.*"

The air snaps between us. This has become a defining moment in our relationship, but it's one I think, deep down, we both knew was inevitable.

"Would tonight count as our first date?" She still hasn't opened her eyes.

"That depends. Do you kiss on your first dates?"

Her eyes finally snap open, and I'm met with a lust-filled gaze. Damn, I've never seen this look on her, but now I don't ever want to see her without it. "Sometimes, I do."

"Well, if you want a kiss good night, then we can count this as our first date. Otherwise, tomorrow can be our first date."

The rise and fall of her chest becomes noticeable as her breathing intensifies. She squirms, and I realize she's turned on. Part of me wants her to say no, this isn't our first date, because I'd love for it to be special to her. But another part of me wants to take her mouth with mine and kiss her until morning.

"Are you a good kisser?" she whispers, inching even closer to me. Bexley watches intently as I lick my lips ever so slightly, moistening what I want to give her.

"I've never had any complaints, but there's always a first time for everything." I cup the back of her neck and pull her closer to me—so close, she's only a whisper from my lips. "It's your call. What do you want to do?"

She moves forward and presses her lips tentatively against mine. In the course of every relationship, there is a make-or-break moment, and this one is ours—I feel it to my core as her apricot scent envelops me. I'm a lost cause.

"First date it is," I whisper against them before wrapping my free arm around her waist and pulling her even closer.

As my tongue slides against her lips, she whimpers so sweetly I want to devour her. We kiss chastely a few times as we begin to find our rhythm. When she opens her mouth for more, I dip my tongue in slowly, needing to savor each millisecond of this moment in time. I'm going to remember this night for years to come.

Our mouths move together as our tongues meet in tandem, and this kiss obliterates any other kiss I've ever had. She moves her hands to my shirt and clutches onto it as if her life depends on me. A sense of pride surges through me at the thought. If there's one person I want to depend on me, it's Bexley.

Her whimpers increase as our kiss deepens, and when she slides her hands up my shirt, I can't hold back the growl that escapes me. There is no doubt in my mind I could kiss her like this until sunrise, but that wouldn't be first-date appropriate. Not the kind of first date she deserves anyway.

As much as it pains me to do so, I bring my hands to her cheeks and slow the moment down. It's for the best. If we keep going, we may end up naked between the sheets, and that's not my goal. Not this week anyway.

"Tristan." She gasps for air as our foreheads remain touching.

"Bexley." I'm equally breathless.

"Are we . . . I mean . . . that was . . . beyond words."

"Good end to our first date?"

She sighs softly, her breath caressing my lips. "Best end to the best first date ever."

"That's high praise, coming from you."

She giggles, and it's the sweetest sound. "So are there kisses at the end of the second date?"

The eagerness in her voice is exactly what I hoped to hear. "If we play our cards right, there very well could be."

"Do you have it planned already?"

I pull back slightly so I can see her eyes. "I was thinking we could wake up and plan it together?"

She's been out on so many dates. I don't want to do anything repetitive or associated with bad memories, but most of all, I think Bex would enjoy having a say instead of the constant way she stresses about what to wear and if she'll like what the men in her life do.

Her smile confirms I was right. "I'd love to plan something together. Thank you."

She yawns, and after last night, her long day at work, and the drinks she had at the bar, I know she's sleepy. I stand and hold out my hand, which she eagerly takes. "Let me walk you to your door."

I've held Bexley's hand a thousand times, but this time is different. This is the time I'll always remember. "Can you do me a favor?"

When she looks up at me, her eyes dance with happiness. "I'll try."

"When we go out on our dates, and I inevitably do something that lands me on your naughty list, come home and write it down. But for every one strike against me, I want you to make a note of five things I do right."

She cracks a grin but easily agrees. "Okay."

"Thank you," I reply, before sliding a finger under her chin and tilting her head up. My mouth covers hers, and my tongue dips inside for one last brief taste of her until next time. "Good night, Bex. Sweet dreams."

"Night, Tristan."

Five

Bexley

When I finally make my way into the kitchen, it's after ten in the morning. I haven't slept as well as I did last night in a long time. There are fresh donuts on the table and coffee in the pot.

Once I've got the perfect ratio of cream and sugar in my cup, I open the box of donuts and groan.

I'm going to have to go to the gym if I eat these, but there's no way I'm not eating these. I pull two of my favorites onto a paper towel and lose myself in memories of last night's kiss.

Over the years, there have been times when I've wondered what it would be like with Tristan. There would be something incredibly wrong with me if I didn't. He's kind, loyal, and giving. He's a serial monogamist and dates with purpose—not just for sex. Occasionally, he'll have a one-night stand, but they're the exception – not the rule. Plus, with his caramel-colored curls and his blue eyes, not to mention a dimple to die for and the chiseled jaw of a runway model, the man is gorgeous. He's confident and cocky, but not in a bad way, and he would do anything for the people he cares about.

So yeah, of course, I've thought about being with Tristan, but once I get past all the plus sides of a potential relationship with him, I arrive at the negatives. Not negatives like tasseled shoes; negatives like screwing everything up and losing him from my life forever.

Even though we shared a life-altering kiss last night, I'm not prepared for a reality without him. It's too late to second-guess myself now. Sure, he'd let me back out, but I don't want to be that fearful girl anymore. I want to be the kind of woman who deserves a man like him.

"Hey," Tristan says as he towels off in the doorway. Sweat drips down his forehead, and his abdomen glistens before he wipes the perspiration away.

"Way to make me feel like a slob. You left me here with my biggest weakness, and you've been out running."

His laughter lights me up, and fuck, that smile has a sinful effect on my lady parts. "Didn't you notice there were already four missing? If I hadn't gone for a run, you'd have to roll me out to our date tonight."

Tristan doesn't actually like running, but he does it when he's anxious or when he needs to process something. He says once he hits his stride, it's like his mind goes into fast-forward, and when the endorphin rush kicks in, everything begins to make sense.

"Why did you go for a run?" *Please don't say it's because you regret last night.*

He steps forward and tilts my head toward him, pulling my gaze from the inside of my coffee cup. "Because it was the only thing keeping me from waking you up and kissing you good morning."

"Oh." That was unexpected.

"You're welcome."

"Who says I would have minded?"

He grabs a water bottle from the refrigerator and chuckles. "Bex, I'm going to try my damnedest to follow appropriate date protocols for the next six dates." Then he leans down, his lips ghosting over the shell of my ear, and in that sexy fucking tone, he lights my soul on fire. "If we make it to an eighth date, I'm not going to be a gentleman. On date number eight, I'm going to make you beg, and you're going to love every fucking minute of it."

I have no words. Literally none, and I don't need any as he leans down and kisses the top of my head. "I'm taking a shower. We'll talk about what you want to do tonight when I get out."

Once I hear the shower turn on, I ditch my coffee and donuts and dash to my room. I find an unused notebook and open it, then title seven pages with date numbers. After drawing a dividing line on each one, and labeling the top half of the page *good* and the bottom half *bad*—I'm ready to begin.

For now, I skip the first date page and go straight to the one assigned to our second date.

In the good part, I write the first of five good things.

Turned me on in a way I've never been turned on before. I don't know where this version of Tristan has been hiding, but damn . . . I can't wait to get to know him.

Before closing the notebook, I add one more thing.

Brought me donuts this morning—my favorite ones.

When I make it back to the kitchen, I top off my coffee and curl up on the couch to drink it. I'm pretty sure I know what I want to do tonight on our date, but I'm also pretty sure Tristan will laugh at me.

My phone rings, and Rita's picture flashes on the screen. I pick up and put my coffee down. "How did your date go?"

She laughs. "Good morning to you too. I'm just crawling into bed now."

"I take it that means your night went well."

"Mmmhmm, that man has skills."

I don't want to think about Adam's skills. "Must be all the porn he watches."

"I know, right? He's got the perfect job. I'd almost be jealous if I wasn't reaping the benefits of his profession."

She is something else. "Are you going out again?"

Rita yawns. "We are. Tomorrow night, he's taking me to dinner."

Wow. That's a big step for Adam; he must really like her. "That's great. I'm happy for you."

"Thanks. I'm so tired, but I wanted to know what happened with you and Tristan last night."

My coffee goes down the wrong pipe, and I cough. "What do you mean?" I manage to choke out.

"Oh, come on, Bexley! He looked like he wanted to devour you. I'm talking about him-diving-under-the-table-and-burying-his-face-in-your-panties kind of devour. That man wants to claim you, girl, and with that kind of sexual promise hovering in the air between you, you should let him and enjoy every goddamn second of it."

My cheeks are flaming hot. "It didn't get that far."

She squeals. "But it did get somewhere?"

"Maybe . . ."

Tristan chooses this moment to join me on the couch. The scent of his cologne wraps around me and makes me want to climb him like he's a jungle gym.

"He's right there, isn't he? Don't answer that; I know he is. Just tell me, did it go beyond kissing?" Rita asks.

"No, not at all."

"But you did kiss?"

"Yeah, that's great. You guys have a good time."

Rita squeals again and then yawns. Sometimes, she acts like she's still in college, but it's part of her charm. "Monday morning, you're meeting me for breakfast before work. Usual place, usual time."

"You don't have to ask me twice. Chocolate chip pancakes are the best way to start a Monday. But now, I'm definitely going to the gym. Tristan bought donuts for breakfast today too."

"Please, you should go to the gym just so you can pay penance like the rest of us. You have the best metabolism of anyone I've met in my life. Your curves are in all the right places; you're not too skinny, and you're not fat. It's like the body gods saw you and knew you were such a good person inside and out that they made you with zero flaws."

Tristan catches me rolling my eyes and snorts.

"You're being ridiculous. I have more flaws than I can count, but thanks for trying to boost my self-confidence. Get some sleep, and I'll see you Monday." I reach for my coffee and put my phone on the table.

"Did Rita just get home?"

"She did, and apparently, Adam is taking her on a dinner-date tomorrow night." I'm met with a smug grin, and I know what's coming next.

"I told you they'd hit it off."

I reach over and smack his shoulder. "Your inner teenager is showing."

"Like I care. Have you figured out what you want to do tonight?"

"Maybe, but my inner teenager will be showing, and you're probably going to laugh at me."

"I'd never laugh at you, Bex." With an arched brow, I meet his gaze. "Okay, I might laugh at you, but only in fun."

One appealing thing about dating Tristan is that I feel comfortable enough to do things. We already know each other, so we don't have to do all that awkward getting-to-know-you stuff. "What I want to do is very high school but also sort of advanced for me at the same time."

His eyes light up as he grins at me. "I'm waiting."

"This is so embarrassing."

"More embarrassing than the time Adam tripped me in class, and I flew into Mrs. Langley's seventy-year-old rack of triple Ds?"

I laugh so hard I snort through my tears. "That was hilarious, and even though I was mortified for you, I was also happy for her. That had to be the most action she'd seen in years."

He shrugs. "They were comfortable, but most breasts are." He lowers his eyes to mine, and it's suddenly hard to catch my breath. "Tell me what you want to do, Bex."

"Will you take me to the movies?"

"Really? That's it? We've been to the movies a thousand times."

It's now or never. "We have, but I've never made out with anyone in a movie theater before."

I wish there was a way to capture his smile and market it as an antidepressant. There is no way you could look at that grin and not have an endorphin rush.

"Jesus, Bex, how is that even possible?"

"I guess there are a lot of things I've never done. Outside of high school and college, all my dates have been more of the getting-to-know-you kind. Meals, drinks, walks, etcetera, and while we were in school, it was mostly parties and fast food. Movies, sure, but we never got to the making out stage."

God, I wish I knew what he was thinking right now. His expression is blank, and I wonder if I made a mistake by asking for this.

"You know what? It's too much. Never mind—let's just go to dinner."

"No, give me a minute. I'm fighting the urge to do something I shouldn't right now."

"What's that?" I whisper without looking at him.

He groans. "Ask me if we make it to date eight, and I'll show you."

Holy shit.

Six

Tristan

If I look at her, I'm going to pull her onto my lap and fuck her until she's screaming my name. I hate myself for not knowing how innocent Bexley truly is. To be friends with her, I had to let go of certain things. One of those things was a deep interest in her dating life.

In high school, we saw each other all the time, but it wasn't like it is now. We were in the same co-ed dorm in college but on different floors. Between classes and work, we easily maintained our friendship, but it was mostly because of our study sessions and weekend catch-ups.

Moving in together was the logical next step. There wasn't even much of a discussion about it. We'd always kind of joked about getting a place together, and about eight weeks before graduation, Bex showed up at my dorm room with her laptop and a list of apartments.

Once we'd settled in our apartment, everything felt right. I think the only thing she's ever gotten on me about is roaming around naked. We're like two puzzle pieces that fit perfectly. Nothing was ever off-limits except the two of us dating, and because of that, I tried to keep my interest in her dating life minimal. Of course I care, and monitor date numbers and who she's with, but I didn't fish for deeper details. I thought it was the right thing to do, but now . . .

now, I know it's because I couldn't handle hearing the details.

She did the same and kept her distance with my girlfriends. Bex was always friendly, that's who she is, but there was never a time when she went out of her way to join us for movies, or dinner, or anything. In fact, when my girlfriends would stay the night, a lot of the time she would crash at Rita's or she'd stay late at work and go in early. I'd never thought about my love life hurting her or her being uncomfortable, but maybe I should have.

When I open my eyes, hers are locked on me. With a crooked finger, I beckon her closer until her lips meet mine. It's a quick kiss, but it reiterates our connection, and that's what I need.

"What movie would you like to see?" I ask, the taste of her lingering on my lips.

"Does it matter? We won't be watching it." She's cute when she's sassy.

"Okay, I'll get the tickets. I'm trying really hard to respect appropriate dating boundaries, Bex. If you plan to keep pushing them, then I'd suggest wearing a skirt tonight. It's up to you. If you want the high school experience, wear jeans."

She bites her bottom lip as if in contemplation.

"What's wrong?"

"I can tell you anything, right?"

I squeeze her hand in mine, trying to calm her nerves. "Absolutely."

"I don't think I want the high school or the college experience per se."

"What kind of experience do you want?"

The vulnerability in her gaze floors me but not as much as her words. "The boyfriend experience."

Makes sense—it's the one thing she's never had. "Then wear the skirt, Bex. We'll have our dates, but if we're going to skip ahead in the script to boyfriend status, you need to wear the skirt."

She's staring at me with hooded eyes, and my cock is stirring to the point of no return. I've got to get out of here for a few minutes. "I need to do some work. I'll let you know what time the movie is when I get the tickets."

"Okay." Her eyes are a bit unfocused as she answers.

Once I'm safely ensconced in my room, I pull up the local theater and find the smallest auditorium in the place based on the seating charts. As if the movie gods know Bex needs this, no other seats have been sold in there so far. The movie has been out for a while, and it has horrible reviews. Some indie horror flick, which also likely means anyone else going will be there for the same reason we are.

I buy two rows of tickets—the one we'll sit in, the one directly in front of us. It's worth every fucking penny to have Bex alone in a secluded corner of the theater. My teenage self would've loved that kind of space with a date. I'm tempted to buy every seat, but part of the fun is the risk.

After that's taken care of, I pop my head out and tell Bex what time to be ready, answer a few emails, and spend a couple of hours playing the new game and checking for any additional bugs.

I'm just about to start getting ready when Adam calls. "Want to grab some dinner?" he asks.

"Can't. I have a date."

"Do tell. Did you meet her at the bar last night? Is she hot? Big tits?"

Laughing, I answer, "No, yes, and they're perfect for me."

"Why are you being dodgy?"

"I'm not, but I'm also not going to give you tons of details." I toss my controller down and flop back on my bed.

"Well, well, well, you finally did it, didn't you? You're in your very own round of dating roulette."

Now I understand why Bex hates it when I call it that. This isn't a game to me, and I know it's never been a game to her. "It's worse than that, I think."

His snort irritates me. "Did you finally realize you're in love with her?"

I shoot straight up. "What? No!"

"If you haven't yet, you will. I'm pretty sure you've been in love with her since senior prom. Why do you think I tried to put you out of your misery and gave you my permission to date her?"

Senior prom was a hell of a night. Bexley was on a rare date seven. Her date rented a room at the hotel, hoping to take Bex's virginity. When she told him it wasn't on the table, he took off. She went up to the room to try to work things out because she truly liked the guy, and he was already in there fucking someone else.

I'd gone stag, and she spent the rest of the night crying on my shoulder. I held her in my arms until sunrise, and then I took her out for her favorite chocolate chip pancakes.

"Tris, you still with me? Are you realizing I'm right?" Genuine concern fills Adam's normally cocky tone.

"No. Maybe. Fuck, Adam, I don't know. What I do know is that if I don't start getting ready, I'm going to be late for date number two."

"Have fun, man, and enjoy it. You've been waiting a long time for this day to come."

Bex's long, flowing skirt has more than enough room for us to hide a number of sins. I won't push it, not tonight, but I wish I could. She smells like apricots and cream, and I want to lick the inviting scent off her skin.

She didn't want any snacks, only a bottle of water, and as the lights go down and the previews begin, we're the only people in this theater. Her eyes are on the screen as I entwine our fingers together. She whips her head toward me, and I pull her hand to my lips and kiss it.

Leaning in closer, I nip the shell of her ear, and she sucks in a deep breath. That's not good enough. I need her squirming and panting more than I need my next breath. As I trail kisses along her jaw, her shoulders relax.

"What stage of our relationship do you want to be in tonight?" Moving back to her ear, I suck the skin beneath it into my mouth.

"Uh . . . wh . . . what was the question?"

"How about pet names? Do we have them yet?" I ask.

I flick her earlobe with my tongue. "Su ...Sss ... Sure." Her heated response emboldens me to continue.

"Are we fucking yet, Bex? Or are we at the stage where we haven't yet, but we've done almost everything else?"

"Oh God," she mutters, and I chuckle against her skin. The screen lights up as the preview ends and the movie begins. Her nipples are poking against her shirt. What I wouldn't give to be able to suck them into my mouth right now.

She's in the farthest seat against the wall in the darkest corner at the back of the theater. As casually as possible, I slide my hand across her breast, and her head falls back.

"Tristan . . ."

With our fingers still entwined, I pull our hands down to my cock, and she releases the neediest fucking hiss I've ever heard in my life.

"Maybe we should pretend this is the first cock you've ever touched," I say, and she squeezes her legs together as she pushes against me. Releasing her hand from mine, I want to see what she does. Will she pull away, or will she play along?

When I leave her hand in place, she explores my dick with her fingers. She shifts in her chair so our heads are touching. "I've seen you naked. I knew you were on the bigger side, but damn, Tris, I never knew you were blissfully blessed by the gods of peen."

I pull her head closer until my mouth captures hers. I want to devour her body one kiss at a time. As our tongues meet, she squeezes my cock, and I pinch her nipple between my fingers. Her back arches as she presses into me. She wrenches her lips away from mine. "Harder, Tristan, please."

I might come in my pants like a teenage boy, but there's no way I'd deny that request. I turn my head to be sure no one has walked into the theater yet just as the opening credits are rolling. We're still alone for now, which means I can move freely.

"Get on your knees and turn toward me." Her eyes widen, but she immediately complies. "Put your arms around me like we're hugging."

She throws her arms around my neck and breathes softly against my ear. "Like this?"

"Exactly like that." I slide my hands under her shirt and massage her breasts. Her breathing quickens, and the harder I squeeze, the faster her breath hits my skin. When I simultaneously pinch both nipples between my fingers, she bites my neck. More than anything, I want to suck them into my mouth, but I can't do that without exposing her.

With each pinch, I increase the intensity. She rewards me by kissing my neck, licking my skin, and whimpering in my ear.

"Has anyone come in, angel?" I ask. She gives a high-pitched whimper at the pet name. She likes it.

"No." She gasps breathlessly.

"Good, because you've been teasing me tonight, and now it's time for some payback." As I bring my lips to hers, I slip a hand under her skirt. She stifles a cry when my fingers dance along the seam of her silky panties. She's hot and wet in all the best places. I'd rather be doing this with my tongue, but if I play my cards right, my patience will be rewarded.

Our kiss escalates, and I slide my hand into her panties. My fingers glide easily through her excitement, and

D. Kelly

she kisses me deeper as I circle her clit. She's a ball of pent-up sexual frustration, and it's hot as hell. I thrust a single finger inside her, flick her clit, and pinch her nipple in the perfect combination. Bexley explodes, and I swallow her cries as her pussy pulses around my digit. She rides my hand through her orgasm, and I slide my hand out from under her shirt and caress her cheek. As her orgasm subsides, our kiss slows.

"Tristan," she says softly, pulling back from our kiss to look at me.

When I slip my hand out of her panties, she reaches for a few napkins she stuffed in her purse earlier. She watches, eyes locked on mine, as I bring my finger to my mouth and suck her sweet essence from my skin with a tortured groan.

"I can't believe you're doing that right here," she hisses. The theater is still empty, but even if it wasn't, I'd give no fucks at this point.

"And I can't believe I've been missing out on your taste for ten fucking years." With both hands, I pull her face to mine and kiss her like the starving man I am. Our tongues entwine, and my cock aches with the knowledge I'm sharing her flavor with her.

She pulls away, gasping. "This is so damn dirty."

I pull her close until our foreheads touch. "You think this is dirty? Wait until I come in your mouth and then devour your lips after. You can call it dirty, carnal, depraved, but I call it a fantasy fulfilled, and I can't wait."

She bites my bottom lip and soothes the sting with her tongue.

Our sexual chemistry is incredible, but the small part of my conscience that's been whispering to me all night is becoming louder. Bexley isn't a hot hookup for the night—she's someone I could easily see myself building a future with. As sexy as it is to get her off in public, she deserves to know her worth. "Bex, I am sorry. You deserved a much better second date than this."

56

Her fingers lace through my curls, and she tugs my hair gently and smiles. "Are you kidding me? This is exactly the date I wanted. I know we're pretending in a sense, but . . ."

"Hey, this might be a form of pretending, but my feelings are real, and if I make it past date seven, you better bet the boyfriend title is a given. I want you to be mine, Bexley. Now I need to figure out how not to fuck that up."

After placing a brief kiss on my lips, she gets comfortable in her seat and leans her head on my shoulder with a sigh. "That makes two of us. If it helps, you're getting extra credit for the orgasm that was above and beyond."

I want to tell her it wasn't nearly enough, but I don't want her to take it the wrong way. With the taste of her still lingering on my lips and tongue, all I can think about is more.

"Tris," she whispers. "Does it bother you that I'm kind of kinky?"

The kinkier, the better is probably not the best answer right now. "Should it?"

"I'm not sure. I've been with some guys who weren't into it, which was totally fine since all my sexual encounters were one-night stands. But if we were to develop into something more, it's kind of a big deal for me. I, uh . . . enjoy sex more if I'm being challenged."

It makes so much sense. The commanding tone, her appreciation for pain, the way watching turns her on.

"What's your favorite position?" I ask, placing a kiss on the top of her head.

Her eyes flutter closed and then open again. "Any one where my hands are tied, or I'm being restrained."

Ladies and gentlemen, this is my motherfucking soul mate. "Damn it, Bex," I growl as I adjust my dick in my pants.

She looks down and giggles when she sees what I'm doing. "Want me to help you with that?"

Yes, I want you on your knees, hands behind your back, with my dick in your mouth. But that is not a second date action, and I've already screwed up tonight. "Yes, but another time. You being kinky doesn't bother me in the slightest. We'll have to have some conversations down the road, but one thing about me is that you can guarantee if you're turned on, I'm going to be turned on."

Her eyes flare, and she quickly turns her attention to the screen. "Do you have any idea what this movie is about?"

"Not a single clue."

She giggles. "Well, maybe we should spend the rest of it making out. What do you think?"

I give her my answer by pulling her mouth to mine.

Seven

Bexley

After the movie, we went to a late dinner at our favorite Mexican restaurant. Dating Tristan is essentially effortless. Because we have an existing relationship, we get to skip the usual getting-to-know-you awkwardness. Until he looks at me, or brushes his fingers against mine, or kisses me senseless. Then it's a whole new world. I've never felt as alive as I do with him. Even when things should be uncomfortable, like when my very best friend got me off tonight, he made it feel like the most natural thing in the world.

When the check comes, I reach for my purse.

"What are you doing?" he asks with a weary expression.

"Paying my share."

With a narrowed gaze, he shakes his head. "No, you're not. We may have done some improper things tonight, but this is still a proper date."

At first, I think he's joking. "We always go dutch. Let me get my card out of my wallet." I'm digging through my purse when he grabs my wrist and lights every hormone in my body on fire. If it were anyone else, I'd give him hell, but this is Tris, and after our kink talk, I know he's doing this with intent.

Our eyes meet, and he squeezes tighter. Not enough to hurt but enough to make me wish we were somewhere private. "Bexley, I'm not kidding. I asked to date you, and that means anything we do will be my treat. You know money isn't an issue, so put your purse down and say thank you."

My heart races, and I wish like hell this was date number seven. With a slight nod, I say, "Thank you."

He releases my wrist, and I miss the contact immediately. Tristan leans over and kisses me. "You're welcome."

On the way home, I decide to ask him something I've been wondering about for a long time but have never wanted to risk opening the door on. "Hey Tris, how come we still live together?"

Immediately, he pulls the car into an empty parking lot. Once he parks, he faces me. "Why wouldn't we live together? We're both single, we get along great, and we're best friends."

"Right, I know all of that, but you're kind of a big deal these days. Your last three games have made you money beyond your wildest dreams. Don't you want to buy a house? Renting with me seems like a waste for you."

He rakes his fingers through his curly hair, and I'm instantly jealous. I love the feel of his hair in my hands. "You know, Bex, you're not exactly a pauper. Your salary is pretty insane. Why do you still live with me?"

I'm smiling before I even realize it, and with a slight shrug, I tell him the truth. "You're my favorite part of the day. Why would I want to lose that?"

Tris unbuckles his seat belt and leans in, a whisper away from my lips. "And you're the best part of mine. Money doesn't buy happiness, Bex."

My mouth opens before his lips find mine, and it's as if we're a pair of horny teenagers again with a fetish for each other's hair. I'm a disheveled mess when we part, and so is he.

By the time we reach our front door, I'm yawning. Between the orgasm and the margarita at dinner, I'm wiped out.

Tristan walks me to my bedroom door again. It's the sweetest gesture.

"Thank you for the date. I had a really great time." I flutter my eyelashes at him, knowing this is one of his few dating pet peeves. I'm sure he realizes I'm intentionally trying to provoke him. If he wants to command me to stop in that sexy voice of his—it wouldn't be the worst way to end our date.

He steps closer, and we share a long, lingering kiss. His reaction is completely opposite of what I expected, but it turns me on all the same. "It's not so annoying when you're doing the flirting. Do it on date number seven, and you might even be rewarded."

"I'll keep that in mind." I move to step inside my room, and he reaches for my hand.

"Two things—tonight was the best second date I've ever had."

My heart flutters in my chest. Tristan has always been a good guy, and I've always envied his girlfriends for being with someone as incredible as him. But having him turn those charms on me is a bit exhilarating.

"Also, in a little while, if you hear me call out your name, know that I'm reliving the sensation of your pussy clenching my finger and imagining it was my cock instead. Now go make your list from tonight's date while I take care of business."

Holy shit. He *did not* just say that.

I close my eyes and take a deep breath.

"Keep your eyes closed and tell me what you're thinking right now."

"You're cruel for telling me that because all I want to do is make myself comfortable at the foot of your bed and watch."

His lips are against my head, and when I inhale, his cologne seeps into my lungs and settles around my heart. He's starting to imprint himself on each one of my senses in a new and enlightening way. I hope it never stops.

"Bexley, I'm pretty sure that's at least a fifth date opportunity. Imagine it now, and when it happens, you can let me know what's better: the fantasy or the reality. Good night, angel."

"Night, Tris." After closing the door, I lean against it. I was so close to telling him that so far, the reality is beyond any fantasy I've ever had, but I'm not quite ready to put those cards on the table yet.

Once I've grabbed my pajamas, I take a quick shower so I can clean myself off. My nipples are slightly bruised, but knowing Tris is the one who marked me sends a fresh wave of desire coursing through my body. I'm buzzing with excitement as I wrap the towel around myself and step into the hall to go back to my room.

The sound of Tristan moaning stops me in my tracks. He's louder tonight, and when I turn toward his room, I see why. The door is cracked open. Normally, I'd duck into my room, but he never leaves his door ajar. He's not playing fair.

"You enjoy that, don't you?" His words travel into the hall, and I bite my lip to keep from answering.

The combination of his grunts, his breathless moans, and echo of his hand as it glides through the lube as he works himself up has me crossing my legs, hoping I don't spontaneously combust.

"Fuck, Bex, just like that . . . fuck me harder . . . yes, yes, your pussy is so hot, so wet, and so fucking tight."

I'm pretty sure I need another shower now, but as the sound of flesh working flesh intensifies, so do his groans.

"Bexley!" he cries out, and my clit pulses with need. My name on his lips is the sexiest thing I've ever heard. I take a step away from his door because I'm now in desperate need of my vibrator.

"Good night, Bex. Sweet dreams."

"Oh my God," I mumble as my face heats with embarrassment. Tristan only laughs, and I realize it's the happiest he's sounded in a really long time.

I decide to skip getting myself off. Maybe I'll become so needy I'll sleepwalk straight onto his dick instead. After I'm comfortable in bed, I reach for the journal and review what I have for today before adding to it.

Under the good column, I've got the following:

Turned me on in a way I've never been before. I don't know where this version of Tristan has been hiding, but damn . . . I can't wait to get to know him.

Bought me donuts this morning, my favorite ones.

I make the following additions:

Let me listen as he fucked his hand to thoughts of me.

Treated the date as a real official date and paid for everything

Told me I'm the best part of his day. (This one would veto a thousand fuckups)

Bad part of the date:

He wouldn't let me watch him as he got himself off— letting me listen earned some brownie points back.

On Sunday, Tristan and I were like ships passing in the night. We were both up early but for vastly different reasons. He got called into work, and I made myself go to the gym.

I spent the remainder of the day running errands and catching up on laundry. I tried staying awake until he got home but ended up falling asleep on the couch.

Being the gentleman Tristan is, he did wake me so I could have a good night's sleep in my own bed. Or maybe it was so he could kiss me senseless at my bedroom door— either way, I'm not complaining. After an incredible night's sleep, I woke up this morning well-rested and ready for my breakfast date.

Rita passes me the syrup for my pancakes and groans appreciatively as she takes a bite of her own.

"Why don't we start every day with breakfast at Rudy's?" she asks when she swallows.

"Because we'd never be able to leave the gym, and my body can't handle that kind of torture. I'm still aching everywhere after going yesterday."

Her brow arches. "You sure you're only sore from the gym, and you're not holding out on me about Tristan? I mean it's been a while since you've gotten laid. Maybe your body is getting used to being used again."

"Don't I wish." With a sigh, I take a bite of the chocolatey goodness on my plate.

"Would you go there, Bex? Risk everything for a roll in the sack?"

"After the seventh date, yes. Before then, even though it would be incredibly hard to turn down, no."

Rita sips her coffee and flashes me a sympathetic gaze. "Honey, have you ever considered that you could make it past the first seven dates with anyone and the relationship still might not work out?"

"Sure, in the abstract, but it's not something I need to worry about until I can actually make it through all seven dates."

The waitress drops off more cream for my coffee and hands me a note. "Some guy dropped that off and asked me to give it to you. You're a lucky girl; he was a cutie."

"Thanks." Rita watches with rapt attention as I open the note.

Bexley,
One of the perks of being your own boss is making your own hours. For date number three, I'd like to take you to a picnic on the beach. I know I told you to pick the dates, but since this is one of your favorite things, I figured it

would be okay to take control. Let me know if there is a day this week you can get off an hour or two early. I'll handle the rest.

Tristan

"Wow . . ." I pass the note to Rita.

She looks up at me and smirks. "That smile on your face is going to be a permanent fixture soon, isn't it?"

"One can only hope."

"Tristan is one of the good ones. I hope this works out for both your sakes."

She's not the only one. "Me too, but enough about me. How was your dinner with Adam last night?"

Rita points at her eyes. "See these bags? They're from the all-night fuck fest we had after he bought me an amazing meal. Did you know he likes basketball?"

"Yup, he and Tristan were on the team in high school. They still play pick-up games on the weekends with some friends."

"You should show me your old yearbooks sometime. You're lucky you're still friends with people you went to high school with. We moved around so much I never really lived anywhere long enough to make friends I wanted to keep in touch with."

Poor Rita. That had to be difficult. "Considering I could have killed their friendship, I did get lucky. Adam is one of the few who made it to date seven, and then I found out he kissed his ex, and that was that. Stupid high school shit. I met Tristan the day I called it off and decided we should be friends. Best decision of my life."

Rita tosses some money on the table, and I look at the time. I shovel in a few more bites while she nurses her coffee. "They got past it, though, obviously."

I down the rest of my coffee and put my part of the bill and tip on the table as well. "Sure, they fought about it for a brief period — bros before hos and all that. Adam ended up going back to his ex a few days later. She's the one he was kissing—everything was fine after that."

"When did the three of you become friends?" she asks as we walk to our cars.

"The following year, we had some classes together. Tristan and I were like two peas in a pod at that point. Adam spent most of his time with his girlfriend and realized it was easier to bury the hatchet with me so we could all hang out than it was trying to get Tris to ditch me when Adam could squeeze him into his schedule. It was easy to love Adam as a friend. We just weren't compatible as a couple."

I pause as we reach our cars. "Well, that was an early-morning monologue. Sorry for the history lesson—you know I get carried away sometimes. Do you guys have another date set up?"

Rita digs through her purse for her keys. "Yup, he's taking me out Friday night, but I'm hoping for a midweek booty call."

Adam will probably marry Rita. She's literally the female equivalent of himself.

"I'm sure you'll get your wish. We should go before we're late. Have lunch in my office?"

"You know it." She waves, and I pull out my phone. Before pulling into traffic, I sync to the Bluetooth and call Tristan.

"Bexley." His voice is smooth as silk.

"Tristan, should we add stalker to your resume?"

The sound of his laughter greets my ears. I've always loved his laugh. "It's hardly stalking when you run out the door screaming your goodbyes and that you're late to meet Rita at Rudy's."

"That's a very good point."

"You know what would have been better?"

I have a few ideas, but I'll keep those to myself for now. "If I'd invited you?"

"God, no. The last way I want to start my morning is with Rita recapping her all-night sex-a-thon with Adam.

However, a good start to my day would have been a kiss goodbye." His words are the best kind of foreplay.

"Is that so? I didn't realize we'd graduated to morning kisses."

"Bexley, after last night, I think we've graduated to at least that, don't you?"

Damn, I hope so. "Okay, we can do that. I mean, you know . . . add morning kisses to our approved activities."

"I take it you got my note?"

Bless him for changing the subject before I completely soak my underwear before I even get to work. "Yes, and I love the idea of a beach picnic. Unfortunately, I have meetings tonight, dinner with the parents tomorrow, and I'm out of town for that conference on Wednesday and Thursday, but I have Friday off since I'll be traveling most of the morning."

He groans, and it reminds me of the audio performance I got last night. "All right, Friday it is, but it's going to be a long week. Can we schedule dates four and five for Saturday and Sunday now since we're losing the entire week?"

"I'll pencil you in."

"Good and think about what you want to do. I like being able to give you things you haven't had, Bex. Believe it or not, it makes me happy."

I'm pretty sure my heart just grew three sizes bigger. Or maybe I'm suddenly developing an arrhythmia. Whatever the case may be, Tristan Xavier Jacobs is becoming hazardous to my health. "I'll let you know. Have a good day, Tris."

"You too, angel."

Eight

Tristan

"Let me get this straight. Bexley is out of town, and you guys haven't made plans for phone sex? Video sex? Nothing?" Adam opens our beers and passes me one.

"We haven't even had our third date yet."

"Neither have Rita and I, but that hasn't stopped us from screwing each other senseless."

My head whips around at his words. He didn't say fuck. "You really like her!"

Adam picks at the label on his bottle and avoids eye contact. "So what?"

"Nothing. It's cool. I like Rita, and she's a good friend to Bex. What's your plan?"

He finally looks at me. "No plan, just keep dating and having sex. If it's meant to last, it will. What's your plan?"

"Spend the week working, go to the gym, and take Bex out on Friday."

Adam kicks his feet up on the coffee table. "You know that isn't what I was asking. Are you going to marry her or what?"

"It's a little soon for that, don't you think?"

He downs his beer and slams it on the table. "Stop being a dick, Tris. You're dating Bexley, your best friend.

This can go quite a few ways, and most of them are bad. I'm trying to be a friend. Talk to me."

"What do you want me to say? I'm scared shitless this is going to kill our friendship?"

"For starters," he answers with a smug grin.

"You're right; this could go to hell fast. I don't know what concerns me more—not making it through the seven dates, or actually making it through and figuring out what's next."

Adam grabs us two more beers and sits back down.

"For what it's worth, I thought you two would have figured out you were in love with each other before we graduated college. Whatever this is between you has been a long time coming."

I'm in a shit mood, and I know it's because Bex is out of town. I usually miss her when she's gone, but this time, I ache for her. "I would, you know . . ."

Adam watches me in silence while I try to figure out how to put my thoughts into words.

I finish off my first beer and hope I don't regret this. "I'd marry her. In a fucking heartbeat."

"Like I didn't already know that."

"What the hell? Why did you ask then?"

"I wanted to know if you knew it yet."

"Asshole," I mutter, but he only shrugs. "It's not like I want to drop down on one knee and propose right fucking now. When I used to think about the future, I imagined our spouses getting along, our families vacationing together, and our kids growing up to be best friends. It's different now. The future I see has easily shifted to one where she and I are together. It's next to impossible to imagine her with anyone else—and that's how I know I'm fucked."

"Nah, Bex adores you, and she has since she met you. Maybe that's why I'm surprised it took you so long to date. That girl saw you and pulled you straight into her orbit before anyone else had the opportunity."

I toss him a controller so we can play and get past this conversation. "Fifteen-year-old Bex did not have an ulterior motive to get me into bed with her ten years later."

He flashes me a disbelieving gaze before turning his attention to the game. "Maybe not, but she knew she wanted you to be her friend. You've got to admit it's worked well at keeping a large number of women out of your life."

While we play, I think about what he said. I've dated more than my fair share but never as much as him and some of our other friends. In part, it was because I enjoyed my time with Bexley, and I missed her when we spent too much time apart. But there is no way she somehow intentionally created that scenario to have me to herself.

I've taken Friday off as a much-needed vacation day. It also gives me the opportunity to be ready for the beach whenever Bex is home and ready to go. She always hates these conferences, so I've made sure to get some extra wine and her favorite comfort foods.

On the way home from the gym, I picked up her favorite cupcakes. I'm tucking them into the picnic basket when the front door opens.

"I'm in the kitchen!" I don't want her to be scared since I'm home in the middle of the day.

"Hey, what are you doing here?" she greets me with a killer smile.

"Mental health day. How was your trip?"

She stalks toward me and wraps her arms around me. "Much better now."

"Did you miss me?"

Her arms go around my neck, but she's on her tiptoes. I scoop my hands under her ass and lift her as she wraps her legs around my waist. I could get used to this.

"Maybe," she offers, and her lips meet mine. Bexley takes control of the kiss, and I tighten my arms around her while carrying her to the kitchen counter. She keeps her legs around my waist when I set her down, and I pull her hips flush against me. "Tristan." She gasps, breaking the kiss and throwing her head back. She grinds against me as I lick a path from the column of her neck back to her lips.

"I missed you, too," I reply, before crushing my mouth to hers. We've missed ten years of this, and there's no way I want to miss another second of time together. She slides her fingers through my hair as our lascivious kiss deepens. Every whimper of hers fills me with hope for our future.

I hate that she needs these dates to accept what I already know – we're meant to be. But for whatever reason, that validation is important to Bex, and if it brings her to the same page as me, I'm in.

The two of us kiss for what seems like forever before she finally pulls away. "I missed our good morning kisses," she confesses quietly.

"I missed kissing you good night at your door."

She leans forward and catches my earlobe between her teeth. "I really missed the sound of my name falling from your lips as you come."

With a groan, I steady myself against the counter. "I missed taking you out on dates so we could be closer to date eight. I'm looking forward to calling out your name when your sweet pussy clenches around my cock."

"Holy fuck, Tris. Tonight, can we pretend we're on date eight?"

I pop a quick kiss on her lips and grab us both some water from the fridge. "No way. You have a process, and there's not a chance in hell we're going to skip dates, no matter how much I want to."

"Fine." She's pouting, but she's cute as hell when she pouts. "Then I need a nap because no matter how nice the hotel is, I don't sleep well alone."

"You sleep fine here."

"That's because you're here. I always sleep better where you are."

I lift her off the counter and hand her the water. "Go sleep. When you wake up, I'll bring your suitcase in for you. Whenever you're ready, we'll head out. No rush."

She squeezes my hand. "I'm really glad to be home, Tris."

And before I can return the sentiment, she's gone.

"Why did you let me sleep so long? It's almost dark!"

We're in the car on the way to the beach, and Bex is still mad. I reach for her hand and pull it to my lips for a kiss.

"Relax. The beach is better at night, anyway. We can eat under the stars. I brought some lanterns, or we can build a fire."

"I feel bad. You took the day off and everything." She crosses her arms over her chest and slumps down into the seat.

"Yup, and I caught up on all of my geeky superhero shows that were clogging the DVR. It was great. I haven't had a day to be a couch potato in I don't know how long. It was a win for us both; you got some much-needed rest, and I got to get my geek on."

Bexley giggles and laces her fingers in mine. "Well, I do know how much you love letting your inner geek out. Plus, you're right—the beach is gorgeous at night."

We find a strip of beach that doesn't have any people right now and set up our stuff. We manage to catch the tail end of the sunset.

She turns toward me, wearing a beautiful smile. "Watching the sun go down will never get old."

"Neither will eating dinner under the stars with you."

"Damn, Tris, are your lines this smooth for all your dates?"

"Uh, no, actually. Huh." They're really not. I'm not a perfunctory boyfriend by any means, but the way I am with Bex is all because of who she is and who we've always been together.

"What does the 'huh' mean?"

We settle onto the blanket, sitting across from each other. "I think I'm different with you. What do you think?"

She crinkles her nose disdainfully. Maybe that's not a fair question to ask, but she brought the subject up. "Well, I always thought you seemed like a great boyfriend, but I also never really stuck around when you had girls over. I'll just have to take your word for it that it's different with me."

I open the picnic basket and pull out the wine.

"Score one for you."

"Just wait; there's more." After pouring us each a glass, I tug the blanket between us until I've pulled her closer and our knees are touching. "I thought about that the other day. I'm not sure how I never realized whenever I had a girl around you would make yourself scarce."

She lowers her eyes. "It was no big deal."

"Why did you do it?"

Bex sighs. "If you would have asked me this back then, I would have said to give you privacy. But now, I think maybe I knew if I stayed, it would be too hard to witness. Which is stupid because I had no reason to be jealous. But the other night . . ."

Our eyes lock. I've been dying to know what sparked her into action. "What about the other night?"

"The pizza girl. I'd had those drinks, and she was talking about how you never called her again, and I was jealous, Tris. For no reason. I don't get to be jealous of your past, and it's not like I haven't had my share of one-night stands."

She finishes her wine and holds out her cup for more. Once I've filled it for her, I pull out some grapes and then give her a confession of my own. "I hate every guy you go out with except the one-night stands. Those guys fulfill a need for you that I understand, and I know you won't ever see them again. But the guys you date—I think deep down I've been scared that each one will be your guy."

"Why does that scare you?" She leans closer as if she's afraid to miss a word.

"Because I think your guy is supposed to be me."

She sticks her cup in the sand, and straddles my lap. Cupping my cheeks in her hands, she kisses me reverently. "I'm pretty sure he's supposed to be you too."

As quickly as she crawled into my lap, she tries to move off, but instead, I open my legs, and she sits between them as we both face the ocean.

"Tris, do you think we're making a mistake?"

"No."

"What if it doesn't work between us?"

The apricot and cream scent of her mingles with the ocean, and I don't ever want to imagine a time when this isn't my favorite scent. "Then we meet at Rudy's every Saturday without fail until we hash things out, right the wrongs, and recover our friendship."

"Because there isn't anything between us that can't be said over chocolate chip pancakes," she murmurs, and I kiss the top of her head.

"Exactly. Now tell me, have you thought about our next two dates?"

"I have, and tomorrow night is as much for me as it is for you. I want another boyfriend experience, so I got us tickets to Knott's Scary Farm."

"Seriously? It's Halloween; that's the best night to go! We're going to have a blast."

She snorts. "We'll see. I'm still not hip to being scared to death, which is why it needs to be a boyfriend experience. You need to hold me and save me. Or at the very least, wipe away my tears and not laugh at me when I pee my pants."

"How about I do all of the above?"

"Deal." She grabs the extra blanket from under the lantern and wraps it around us.

"If we make it to date five?"

"What do you mean if?" She looks over her shoulder at me.

"Assuming I don't commit an unforgivable sin at the amusement park tomorrow night. Is that better?"

"Slightly, but date five is sort of my revenge. We're having dinner and family game night with my parents."

"Okay." I look toward the picnic basket and feel my stomach grumble. I can't be the only one famished. "Are you hungry?"

"Starving, but really ... you don't mind a date at my parents' house?"

I scoot back so I can make us each a plate without making Bex move and lose the warmth of the blanket. "They're your family. Of course I don't mind."

She nods thoughtfully but doesn't say a word. I'd give anything to know what was going on in her head tonight.

"This is amazing—all my favorites. Thank you." Bexley gifts me one of her sweetest smiles as she takes her plate, and I can't help but wonder what she'll gift me when she sees dessert.

While we eat our dinner under the stars, she fills me in on her time away. Meetings, room service, repeat, and then she drops the bomb.

"We have a new guy who was at the conference too. He's being transferred from the Atlanta office. A group of us got together for drinks after the last day of meetings. The two of us were the last two left at the bar, and he asked me out on a date."

It stings she didn't tell me about this earlier, but Bex is a gorgeous woman; she's going to get hit on for the rest of her life.

"What did you say?"

75

D. Kelly

A hurtful expression flickers across her face. "That I was seeing someone."

"Good."

"There's a catch, though, Tris. Before the conference, my boss asked me if I would take the new hire out, show him the town, and introduce him to the area. I wanted to make a good impression, so of course I said yes. I can't take it back now; I have to spend two nights this week showing Finn around."

What can I say? This is her job, and it's not like I can tell her no. She's been working hard for a promotion, and I know she deserves it. I don't want to be a dick—I'm not that guy—but knowing he asked her out fucking sucks. That means he's attracted to her, so he's likely to try to wiggle his way into her life, boyfriend or not. And that's it in a nutshell; I'm not her boyfriend. Right now, I'm nothing more than her third date.

"Talk to me, Tris, please."

"You're still planning on finishing our dates, right?"

She scoots closer. "Are you kidding? You have no idea how excited I am about our upcoming dates and the future beyond."

Okay, I can handle this. He's probably just some young guy, a recent college graduate, and I've got nothing to worry about. "Speaking of excited, I brought you something else. Close your eyes."

Bex eagerly complies, and I pull one of the cupcakes from the basket. "Keep them closed." I run my finger through the frosting and paint her lips with it. "You can lick your lips now."

Her tongue darts out and slowly tastes the flavor on her lips. She hums in appreciation but keeps her eyes shut. "You bought my favorite cupcakes."

"I did."

"Tris, cover your lips in frosting, put the cupcake back, and come let me devour you under the stars."

She lies down with her hands behind her head, and her eyes remain closed. My dick twitches at the sight of her, and I do as she requested. I position myself between her legs and lower my mouth to hers. Our lips touch and her tongue darts out, eagerly licking the flavor from my lips.

My hips reflexively move, bringing us closer together in the best possible place. As we kiss, she keeps her hands up behind her head, and I catch her petite wrists in my hand and pin her down.

"Shit, Tris, tighter, please."

As I squeeze them tighter, I lower my mouth to her nipples and bite them through her shirt. She cries out, and I take a quick glance around, but we're still the only ones on the beach. The waves crashing against the shore are almost enough to mute her cries — no one needs to hear her desire but me.

She writhes against my body each time I bite, kiss, suck, or squeeze. If she keeps this up, I'm going to come. "Tristan, I need you."

"I'm right here, angel."

"Please, I need to hear you call my name. I want you to, I want us both to . . ."

Fuck me, I want it too.

I sit up and pull her into my lap so she can position herself in the way that feels best. "Put your hands behind your back, Bex."

Her breathing intensifies, and I hold her wrists again. "Work for it, angel. Make yourself feel good and take me with you."

With wide eyes, she nods and leans forward, catching my bottom lip in her teeth. Her hips begin to cant slowly, and she teases me by dipping her tongue into my mouth at the same slow pace.

She started this, but the sad fact is I want her too much to last for long. I've got one free hand, and I use it to wrap her hair around my wrist. Her hips begin to move quicker, and her kiss becomes frantic, practically desperate.

"Tighter," she cries out, and I yank her hair hard enough to loosen our kiss and expose her neck. "Tristan!" she screams when I bite her sensitive skin.

I got caught up in the moment and bit her pretty hard. "That's going to leave a mark."

"I fucking hope so," she pants as she rides my dick through my clothes. "I want you, Tris, no barriers, skin on skin. Make me yours, Tristan . . . for—God, yes!" Her body thrashes against mine again and again as she comes.

"Bexley!" I call out her name, and she pushes against me harder as my cock pulses with my orgasm.

I want this for the rest of my life. There's no going back—not anymore.

I release her hands and her hair and wrap my arms around her. With careful precision, I lay us down on our sides, still entwined with each other. We share kiss after promise-filled kiss under the stars, and I fall deeper in love with my best friend.

Nine

Bexley

I didn't stop smiling the entire way home. Tristan was a true gentleman and let me have the first shower. I tried to convince him we should take one together, but he insisted that was a committed relationship move.

I'm ready to throw this dating bullshit out the window. It feels like a ridiculous thing for us to be doing at this point. Tristan and I have basically been dating for the last ten years. We're like two kids who just discovered sex. When he came beneath me tonight, I almost slipped and told him I wanted him forever. I do, but it's way too soon for him to know that. I don't want to send the guy running for the hills. Not when I've finally found the one.

I exhale slowly as I brush my hair. He's my one. I know it beyond a shadow of a doubt. Maybe subconsciously I knew it the day I told him we should be friends. No one makes me laugh like Tris, and no one has ever made me feel as safe as I feel when I'm with him. He knows I'm looking for love and that I want kids in a few years. The fact that he still wants to date me, knowing all that, gives me hope.

While he's in the shower, I'm going to get down the good and bad things from the date like he asked.

In the good column tonight:

Took me to my favorite place

D. Kelly

Bought all of my favorite foods

Called me Angel multiple times—I think I like this nickname

Got rough with me in all the best ways. He even marked my skin, and God help me, I wish he'd done more of it

Let me ride him till we both came. This is the highlight of my year so far. Having Tristan pulse beneath me as my name fell from his lips was the greatest sexual experience of my life to date.

Now onto the bad . . .

The look on Tristan's face when I told him Finn asked me out and that I was the one who would be showing him around town was heartbreaking. Tristan, I don't know if you're actually going to read this, but I promise you, nothing will happen. I am utterly and hopelessly in love with my best friend. That's you, in case you were wondering.

There's a knock on my bedroom door, and I quickly close my journal and toss it aside to let him in.

"Hey." Tristan's got a shy smile, and his dimple is on full display. I wish I could lick it without seeming creepy.

"Hey, yourself."

"So, tonight I came in my pants in front of a girl I'm dating. It was pretty hot but also extremely embarrassing. Do you think she'll keep our next date? Or should I get used to self-fulfillment again?"

I pull him into my room and motion for him to sit on the bed with me. It's easier to kiss him when we're eye level.

With our lips a whisper from each other, I give him my honest answer. "That's funny. I went on a date tonight, and I came in my pants too. It was by far the greatest sexual high I've ever had. He left bruises on my skin, and I wish he'd given me more. I want to be *his,* but I'm not sure he feels the same. Do you think I've scared him away?"

"Fuck no," he growls and pulls my hair back, taking a long look at the base of my neck. "Damn, that's incredibly hot." He bites me again, and this time sucks my skin into his mouth relentlessly. Thankfully, it's low enough no one at work will see it, but whenever I shower or change my clothes, I'll see it and think of him.

"Tristan . . ."

"Yes, angel?" He kisses a path to my lips and waits patiently for my reply.

"I'd never cancel a date with you. Not ever."

Our lips meet again, and this time, our kiss is slow and sweet. He takes his time exploring my mouth and my lips, all while continuing to steal my heart. When he stands, I want to beg him to stay, but I don't. It's not our time. Not yet.

"Good night, Bexley." He kisses my lips one last time.

"Good night, Tristan. Sweet dreams."

"That was ridiculous! I'm never going to be able to sleep again. How do you love this so much?"

We're driving home after our night at the amusement park. I've never liked being scared, and I just endured seven hours of constant fear. It was also seven hours of being tucked into Tristan's arms as if I was his prized possession, and that's something I could get used to. In fact, it made the entire night worth it.

"It was incredible. Thank you for taking me. It wouldn't have been nearly as fun without you. Having you in my arms all night was much better than going with Adam and playing wingman as he trolled for chicks desperate for help."

"That's so . . . Adam." I'm laughing; I can't help it.

"Yup, he's one of a kind, but maybe he's changing. I think he's into Rita."

I lean back in my seat with a yawn as I flip on the seat warmer. "I'm pretty sure the feeling is mutual. We should have hooked them up ages ago."

"We should have hooked ourselves up ages ago," he adds wistfully.

"Maybe, or maybe this was the perfect time for it to happen."

I don't remember falling asleep, but the next thing I know, Tristan is carrying me to the door. "Why didn't you wake me up?"

He smiles down at me. "You looked so peaceful. I didn't want to disturb you."

"That's sweet, but you're going to have to put me down so you can open the door."

"I would have figured it out," he mumbles as he sets me down. A cat screeches from the bushes, and I jump about ten feet off the ground. Okay maybe three, but after monsters, zombies, and vampires chasing me all night, it's to be expected.

He reaches for my hand and pulls me close. "Relax, Bex. We're home, and you're safe."

The apartment is dark, and I cling to him. He chuckles but doesn't complain. When the lights go on, I breathe a sigh of relief, but I know I'm not going to sleep tonight. This calls for desperate measures.

"Tristan, I need a favor. I know things have changed, and it might not be as easy as it used to be, but, um, could you, maybe ... you know ... sleep with me tonight?"

His raised brow makes me realize how that sounds.

"As friends, in our clothes, like old times. But not like old times because it won't be as easy but—" I blow out a frustrated breath. "Please?"

"I'd be happy to sleep with you and hold you all night, but for the record, Bex, it was never easy."

Well, how about that?

"Thank you."

Tristan kisses my cheek. "Anytime. Go get changed, and I'll meet you in your room. No skimpy lingerie or I'm not going to be able to do it."

"Got it. Skimpy lingerie is at least a seventh-date accessory."

I close the door behind me and quickly throw on a pair of sweats and an oversized T-shirt. I want to use the bathroom and brush my teeth, but I need to update the date journal first.

Good parts of the night:

Spending ninety-five percent of our date in Tristan's arms might have made this the best date I've ever had.

Experiencing his protective nature, even against fake monsters, was incredible. He makes me feel loved.

He fed me funnel cake and didn't ask to share. This makes him my soul mate—I'm sure of it.

Even though he could have, he didn't tease me. Tristan was happy to be there, and I'm pretty sure he was happy to be there with me.

The best is yet to come because I'm about to sleep wrapped in his arms.

Bad part of the night:

These are getting harder and harder to come up with, but I guess I'd say it's right now. Looking for flaws where there are none is tedious. Tristan might not be perfect, but he's perfect for me. I think I've known that since the day we met. He made me laugh, and when I did, his smile became my addiction. A world without Tristan and his smiles would be a world I wouldn't want to live in.

Tristan knocks, and I quickly close my notebook and put it on my desk before letting him in. He's in a pair of flannel pajama pants and a T-shirt. It doesn't really matter what he wears; Tristan is always sexy to me.

"Come on in. I need to use the restroom real quick. I'll be right back." I dart into the restroom and relieve my bladder, wash my hands and face, and brush my teeth in record time.

Once I'm back in the bedroom, Tristan motions to the bed.

"So how do you want to . . ." This is ridiculous. I can't even find my words around him anymore. We've done this a thousand times before—*at least.*

With a sly grin, Tris pulls down the blankets and climbs into his side of the bed. Well, his usual side. "Same as always, Bex. Relax. Nothing is going to happen."

"Maybe that's the problem," I mutter, and he chuckles as I flip off the lights. Even though it's dark, we're facing each other, and he reaches out to caress my cheek.

"Why is it a problem?"

Releasing a sigh at the tenderness of his tone, I scoot closer to him. "I feel like we're going through the motions because we have to. Aren't you tired of the dates?"

"You want to stop? Damn, and here I thought we were having a good time."

"No, rewind. I don't want to stop; I just want . . . more."

Tris wraps his arm around my waist and pulls me flush against his body. "Angel, I want everything with you. But it's important to me to see these dates through, and whether you admit it to yourself or not, it's even more important to you."

"It's really not—"

"Stop. It is. This is your process, Bex, and I don't want you to look back one day and be angry with yourself for not completing it. In the scope of things, seven dates are nothing. We have three dates left, and I'd like to make the most of them."

Before I can stop myself, I'm yawning. Tristan lowers his lips to mine and kisses me with a sweetness that leaves me breathless every time. "Good night, angel."

"Good night, Tris."

Ten

Tristan

First thing after leaving Bex's bed this morning, I hopped in the shower and took care of my needs quietly. I didn't want her waking up to the sounds of me masturbating. At some point, she may think all I want her for is sex. It couldn't be further from the truth, but something about this new part of our relationship has me ready to go all the time.

Once Bexley has woken, showered, and had coffee, we're finally ready for our weekend trip to the grocery store. We've got our routine down to a science, which usually makes shopping easy. That is until I see her reaching for the store-brand cereal.

"What do you think you're doing?"

Her hand hovers over the shopping cart with the generic Fruit Loops and Cocoa Krispies.

"Shopping?" Her high-pitched reply and her red cheeks are enough to make me want to smile. But since Bex likes the controlling part of my personality, I figure maybe I can have some fun with her.

Crossing my arms, I narrow my eyes. "Put those back and get the right ones."

She bites her lip and brings one ankle over the other, crossing her feet. There is something insanely hot about turning her on in the middle of the store. "These are cheaper, Tris."

Stepping completely into her space, I pull the bags from her fingers. She's pressed between me and the shelf. As I push the bags back onto the rack, I nip her ear with my teeth. "You know money isn't an issue anymore, especially when it comes to our guilty pleasures."

Bex whimpers, and my cock jumps. "You . . . you're right, Tris. Won't happen again."

To anyone who doesn't know her, she would almost sound scared, but that's not the case at all. She's so incredibly turned on I'm tempted to abandon the cart and take her to the car for a heated make-out session.

"Bexley, is that you?"

Her eyes dart over my shoulder and widen. *Fuck.*

"Are you okay?" The man sounds concerned.

Any excitement is gone as I step back, losing our connection. She pastes on a smile and steps around me as I put the right cereal in the cart.

"I'm fine, what are you doing here?" she asks.

It's hard not to roll my eyes, but I give her some grace because she's obviously flustered. When I turn around, the man she's talking to eyes me suspiciously. Who the fuck is he?

"Shopping. I live around the corner and figured I should probably stop eating takeout before I have to hire a trainer to get back into shape," the man says.

She laughs flirtatiously. "That's probably a good idea. Finn, meet my roommate and best friend, Tristan. Tristan, this is Finn. I told you about him the other night."

I offer my hand, which he shakes aggressively, like an asshole. "Nice to meet you."

"Likewise," he replies, turning his attention back to Bex. "Are we still on for tomorrow?"

I'm irritated about multiple things, so I interrupt them. "Bex, I'm going to finish shopping. Catch up whenever you're ready." I flash her a smile, hoping it covers my irritation, and take off.

Suddenly, dating her seems like a really bad decision. I've never been a jealous person, but when she introduced me as her roommate and best friend, I felt almost invisible. Jealousy seared through me. Why didn't she tell him I'm the guy she's dating? Probably because she was too busy flirting with him.

By the time she catches up to me, my mood isn't any better.

Bex looks down at the groceries. "You're buying wine?"

I've just added a couple of bottles to the cart. "For your parents. We're still going tonight, right?"

She reaches for my wrist and squeezes it. "Thank you. They'll love it."

"No problem. I think I have everything, but you should probably double check."

Bexley stretches on her tiptoes and kisses my cheek. "I'm sure you have it all; you've never let me down before."

Until about fifteen minutes ago, I would have been able to say the same about her.

Our drive home is mostly silent. She tries to make small talk, but I'm not in the mood to keep it up. After we put the groceries away, I turn to leave the kitchen, the air still heavy between us when she grabs my arm.

"Why are you angry with me?" The sadness in her voice makes me feel like a jackass, but I'm not the only one at fault. She's the one who pretended I didn't exist to the man who's been hitting on her.

"It's nothing. I need to get some work done and maybe catch a nap."

She releases my arm only to immediately wrap her arms around my waist. Bex rests her head on my back. "Whatever I did, I'm sorry. Can we please talk about it?"

Talking about it is the last thing I want to do, but if we let this fester, it's going to get worse. I pull out of her embrace and turn to face her. "You were awfully flirty with Finn today."

Her expression quickly morphs from confusion to amusement. "Tristan, are you jealous?"

"Should I be?"

Her brow furrows as she takes me in. She steps toward me, but I take a step back. "Never. Why would you even think that?"

She's hurt. Maybe I'm blowing this out of proportion. "Why didn't you tell him I was the guy you're dating? The guy hit on you, Bexley, but instead of saying, 'This is Tristan, we're seeing each other,' you said this is my roommate and my best friend."

Her eyes fill with tears, and she nods. "I hurt you. That wasn't my intention at all. You *are* my best friend and roommate, and I've been introducing you to people that way for years. What we have between us is new, and I didn't know in that exact moment what to call us."

"It's not that hard."

A tear slips down her cheek. "Maybe not for you, but this is big for me, Tris. I've been seeing people for years, or dating people—whatever you want to call it. I told Finn I was seeing someone at the conference because I wanted him to back off, but I don't want you to be someone I'm 'seeing.' To me, that feels like I would be degrading what you are to me.

"But I can't exactly call you my boyfriend either. Whatever this is between us, it's so much more than I've ever had before. Excuse me for not being able to define it to a stranger in the supermarket!"

Fuck, I didn't even consider her dating history. I reach for her, and she takes my hand. Using my free one, I wipe away her tears. She sniffs, and I bend down and kiss the top of her head before leading her to the couch.

Taking a seat first, I pull her down into my lap. "I'm sorry, Bex. I was lost in my own head. If the occasion comes up again where you have to introduce me to someone new, especially someone who wants to fuck you, feel free to play the boyfriend card."

"He doesn't want to screw me."

Our eyes meet, and she flips around to straddle me. "You're fooling yourself. That man wants you, and he seems like the kind of guy who doesn't stop until he gets what he wants."

I'm not an insecure man—never have been. I've never lacked dates or sex. But Finn, that guy is polished. Arrogant but charming. I'm sure women fall for him like crazy. He's a bit older than us, and everything about him screams wealth. He's exactly the kind of guy Bex would go for under normal circumstances.

"He taps his fingers when he's impatient. He constantly checks his phone. And at the conference, instead of just asking a question, he would phrase it in a way that made him seem superior to the people putting on the event. Finn had three strikes against him before he ever asked me out. Can you imagine how many more I'd find? He wouldn't make it past a first date, and even if he could, he's not the man I want in my life. You are." Bexley leans forward and traces my lips with her tongue. She tosses her arms around my neck, and I bring my hand to the back of her head and weave my fingers through her hair. I part my lips for her and take control of the kiss. She tastes like the peppermint mocha coffee she drank at the store, and I groan as the flavor infiltrates my senses.

"You taste so fucking good," I say, before lowering my lips to her neck.

Just below the collar of her shirt, the mark I left on her a few days ago is fading. I pull her shirt aside and suck her skin into my mouth. She gasps and pulls my hair when I bite her.

"Tristan, please . . ."

"Please what, angel?" I murmur against her skin. She grinds against my aching dick.

"I want you," she pleads breathlessly. She cries out when I pull her hair, exposing her neck even more.

"No, you can't have me until I know this is real."

"Why?" she pleads, and I thrust against her pussy.

"Because when I finally slide my cock into your sweet little cunt, I'm going to fuck you until we fit together like a puzzle. Your pussy is going to permanently carry the imprint of my dick. But we have to get past our seventh date first. I've never cared about being exclusive with someone before sex. But with you, I don't want to be anything but. Not anymore."

Her mouth crashes against mine, and as our tongues meet, she writhes against me, detonating like a rocket on the Fourth of July. "Tristan!" she cries out, and I slide my hand between us and feel the wetness on the outside of her clothes.

I place a kiss beneath her ear and whisper against her heated skin. "That was so incredibly hot."

"You're a bad influence on me," she says with a giggle.

"I'm the bad influence? I didn't even touch you."

"Mmm, I'm pretty sure your words wrapped around my clit and pushed me over the edge. That masterpiece between your legs rubbing against me didn't hurt either, though." She kills me with her artful references to my body and my cock.

"Maybe on a later date, I can tie you up and test your theory. See just how much I can turn you on with my words and maybe my tongue."

"Your tongue?" Her voice catches, and my dick jumps.

"You have no idea how much I want to lick and suck every inch of your body, Bex. Every. Single. Fucking. Inch."

She leans forward and sighs against my neck. "I can't wait. Tomorrow I have a prior commitment, but on Tuesday, I have a surprise for you. Date six awaits; are you free after work?"

I know prior commitment is code for Finn, but I let it go. She's made it clear he's not the one she wants. "I'll be free whenever you want me to be. The sooner we get to the end of our dates, the better."

"Me too, baby, me too." She yawns, and I'm a bit dazed she called me baby. I think that's a first for her with anyone.

I pull myself to a standing position with her still in my arms and carry her to her room. "Nap, and when you get up, we'll go to game night."

"Sounds good, and if you're free Thursday, we should have our seventh date, then . . ." Her eyes flutter closed as she falls asleep.

I lean down and kiss her cheek. "It would be my pleasure."

My phone chimes a few times in a row on our way to Bexley's parents' house. It rang on our way to the car, but my hands were full, and I ignored it.

I glance over at her quickly. "Can you check that message for me? It could be work so I probably shouldn't ignore it much longer."

She pulls my phone from the center console and punches in my passcode.

Suddenly, Bex is scowling. "It's not your work or Adam. It's Maria."

Maria is an ex from a couple of years ago. "Press play and let's see what she wants."

Bex huffs, clearly irritated, but she complies and syncs the message to the Bluetooth.

"Tristan, you told me to get in touch if I ever decided I wanted to try again. You were right about us. Our chemistry is untouchable, and no matter how hard I try, I've never been able to find the same kind of magic we had. Not even anything comparable. I'm moving back to town next week, and I thought it might be a good time to see if we still have our spark. I'd love to see you, go out on a date, and recreate our magic. What do you say? I checked out your social media pages, and it didn't look like you were seeing anyone; I hope that's still the case. Call me or message me whenever you have time. I can't wait to hear from you."

Holy fucking shit.

"This day just gets better and better," Bex snaps as she disconnects the call and puts my phone back. I reach for her hand, and she pulls it away.

Not willing to go to her parents like this, I pull into a neighborhood park. "Bexley, you can't be mad at me because someone I haven't spoken to in months decided to leave me a voicemail."

She slumps down in her seat and closes her eyes. I know this move. She's trying not to cry. "Maria was the love of your life. It took you a year to get over her. The only reason you broke up is because she moved for her job. I can't compete with that—she was your everything, Tristan. You should call her."

"You're right, I should." I pick up the phone and hit the button to call her. When the phone rings, I hit the speaker button, and when she answers, Bexley's eyes fly open.

"Tristan." Maria's happy tone greets our ears. "I'm so happy you called me back."

"Hey, Maria. Welcome back to town."

"Thank you; I'm excited. I've missed being home and can't wait to be back for good."

Bexley stares at me with a horrified expression. I keep my eyes on hers while I blow Maria off. "I'm sure you have. Listen, the reason I'm calling back so fast is because I wanted to let you know I'm off the market."

"Oh." The disappointment in her voice floods the car. "Is it serious?"

"It's new, but I'm positive it's going to be a long-term relationship."

The sound of her deep, throaty laughter fills the car. Her laugh used to do incredible things to my dick, which is currently flaccid. "How can you know if it's new?"

"Because I'm dating Bexley."

Bexley blinks rapidly as if she can't believe what's happening right now.

Maria sighs but recovers quickly. "Congratulations. I can't say I'm not disappointed, but we both knew that was a long time coming. It's a shame it took you so long to act on it; you guys could have been married by now if you would've made your move when I left." The sadness in her tone is palpable, but so is her understanding.

Bexley's eyes widen. She has no clue how many of my girlfriends thought I was in love with her. They were right—I was just an idiot. What I couldn't see before is clear now, and I'm not about to fuck it up.

I'm not interested in Maria, but I also don't want her feeling bad about herself or our past. "You're selling yourself short. I needed time to get over you. What we had was special, and if you hadn't left, things might have been different. But you did, and I'm happy now. I hope you find your happiness soon."

"Thanks. Maybe the three of us can get lunch one day and catch up. If Bexley would be okay with that. Let me know if you guys want to, but if not, no hard feelings. Bye, Tristan."

"Bye, Maria."

As soon as the call disconnects, Bexley yells at me. "Why would you do that? You were crazy about her!"

I shake my head and put the phone down. "Did you hear that call? I cared for Maria, but I'm crazy about you!"

She launches herself across the console and kisses me relentlessly. When we finally break apart, she shakes her head. "You didn't have to do that."

"We both know I did, and it wasn't a hardship. I've been over Maria for a long time, and I'm definitely not going to mess up the best thing to ever happen to me because she left me an ill-timed message."

Bexley raises her eyes hesitantly. "I thought Maria was the best thing to ever happen to you."

With a sigh, I caress her cheek. "Bex, we've both dated a lot of people. If someone asked me a month ago, out of everyone I'd dated, who I thought I'd end up with, Maria would've been my answer."

"Then—"

"Shh, let me finish. You're my person, Bex, and you have been since the day we met. You, in all your sassy, sexy, frustrated glory—you stole my heart. Exploring this side of our relationship has been the most fun I've had in my life."

"Mine too," she whispers.

"Good, because what I felt for Maria doesn't even compare to how I feel about you. As much as I cared for her, she's the generic cereal in this scenario, and you're the real thing."

"Are you really comparing me to Fruit Loops?"

With a laugh, I kiss her briefly. "I'm saying you're irreplaceable, and there is no substitution in this world for you."

She leans her forehead against mine. "I wish it were Friday, and we were past these dates already."

"Same. Now let's get to game night and show your parents how it's done."

Eleven

Bexley

Maria calling after our fight about Finn threw me for a loop. What are the odds both of us would be confronted by our insecurities on the same day? Between dealing with Finn and Maria, one thing has become clear—Tristan and I are both the jealous type. Finn is a stranger, though, and Maria held Tristan's heart for a long time.

On the outside, Finn is a sexy man. The women and men in our office will be all over him, so I hope someone catches his eye, and he'll back off me. But the difference between Finn and Maria is night and day. Maria is a gorgeous Latina woman with a body to die for. Her skin is flawless, and her hair is perfect even straight out of bed. Beyond the physical, she's one of the nicest people I've ever met. I'm not sure exactly what she does for a living, but I know she's with a non-profit organization that coordinates medical care for kids in third-world countries. She was the love of Tristan's life, and he was devastated when she moved.

"Tris, why didn't you move with Maria?"

He's just parked the car in front of my parents' house. "Because you were here."

My heart races in my chest. It's too soon to say I love him, but it looks like we've both been burying our heads in the sand for a while. "Do you get the feeling we've been wasting time by not dating sooner?"

He smiles and laces our fingers together. "I think our timing is just right. Come on. Your mom is staring at us from the porch."

My mom and dad hug us both as they welcome us inside. Dad ushers Tristan to the family room, and I follow Mom to the kitchen with the wine. She can't stop grinning.

"Say it." I urge her to get it out now before she embarrasses me later.

She rummages through the utensil drawer for the wine opener, and once she finds it, she turns her freaky smile toward me. "He was holding your hand. Care to share?"

"We're dating. Actually, tonight is date number five."

Her hands immediately fly to her hips, and she's in full-on mom mode. "Bexley Marie! Why on earth would you waste a date with your parents?"

"Mom! Hush . . . use your inside voice, jeez. I don't even want the stupid dates anymore. I just want him, but he insists we make it through them all before we can just *be* a real couple. I'm not going to miss a date night because I already promised you I'd be here."

Mom's creepy smile is back. "Why don't you want the dates?"

"You know why."

And the smile widens. Ugh, mothers.

"Do I need to remind you that I've known this all along? In fact, wasn't it before you two went to college that I called how this was going to turn out?" she asks.

I reach for the newly opened bottle of wine and pour some into a glass. "We don't know it's going to turn out how you predicted. We're just testing the waters."

She snorts and proceeds to fill the other glasses. "Testing the waters, my ass. That's the man you're going to marry, Bexley. You didn't believe it then, but you should believe it now. I'm rarely wrong about these things."

"Please don't let him hear you talk like that. You're going to scare him away."

"It would take a lot more than that to scare me away."

I down my wine in three big gulps with his words. Could this get any more embarrassing?

"Tristan, did you know that I told Bexley before the two of you went to college you were her soul mate?"

"Mom! Enough!"

Tristan laughs and pours more wine into my glass. My heated cheeks are a dead giveaway to my level of embarrassment. "Ignore her, Tris, please."

He wraps his arm around my shoulder with a mischievous glint in his eyes. "I don't know, I'm sort of enjoying this conversation. I'm curious, have you been planning your long-term seduction of me since then? Or did it start before?"

My jaw drops as I look up at him. "You did not just say that!"

Mom laughs and winks at him. "I'm pretty sure it started the day she broke up with Adam."

This is not okay. "Dad! Come handle your woman . . . please!"

"Sorry, Bex, it's the fourth quarter, and the Ravens are winning. You're on your own."

Tristan and Mom burst out into laughter, and I finish off the rest of my wine. What was I thinking by bringing him here? They always gang up on me, but this is a whole new level of mortification. "Maybe I should go down the street and hang out with your parents instead," I say.

Tristan leans down and kisses the top of my head. "You could do that. My mom would probably tell you I've been in love with you since high school and used to keep a photo of you under my mattress."

"Did you?" Heat floods my core at even the thought.

"Nope, but if I'd known we'd end up here now, I might have. But my mom may have convinced herself I did. I think it was easier for her to process my teenage habits if they were due to a crush on the girl down the street instead of the women who lived in my computer."

An excited gleam flashes in Mom's eyes. "Masturbation is nothing to be ashamed of. In fact, we told Bexley—"

"Oh my God, Mom, enough! You too." I poke Tris in the chest. "The two of you feed off each other like a bad habit."

Both of their eyes twinkle with amusement. I've always loved how easily Tristan has blended in with my family, and I with his, but them tag-teaming me isn't okay.

"Is it too soon to welcome you to the family, Tristan?" Mom teases. She knows I'm about to lose it, so she grabs her wine and blows me a kiss before joining my dad for the rest of the game.

Tristan squeezes my shoulder gently. "I love your family."

"That makes one of us," I mutter.

Tris pushes my hair aside and lowers his mouth to my neck. "Hush, you love them to pieces. They're why you're such a perfectionist when it comes to love. They're a hard act to follow."

"They are." My admission comes on a sigh.

"I'm almost afraid to know how many strikes I have against me. Are you still writing them down?" The huskiness of his voice has a firm grip on my libido, but I do my best to shake it off and focus.

It amuses me that he thinks he has strikes. Tristan should know better than anyone that if he had irredeemable issues, I wouldn't be able to live with him or be his best friend. Nothing about Tristan bothers me anymore.

"I'm keeping notes of all our dates but so far, so good. You've got nothing to worry about," I reply.

"That's positive."

"Yup."

He spins my barstool around and crouches so we're eye level. "Bex, after the Maria thing—are we still okay?"

"That depends. After the Finn thing, are we okay?"

He chuckles and kisses the top of my hand. "We're quite the pair, aren't we?"

"We always have been."

After a night filled with homemade chili and cornbread, games, laughter, and wine, Tristan and I finally make it home.

We're at my favorite part of date night—when he walks me to my door.

"Why does tomorrow have to be Monday?" I whine, swaying slightly.

"Monday brings us closer to the weekend, and I'm looking forward to this weekend."

That's right—this weekend will bring us to eighth-date territory. "Have you planned date seven yet?"

Tris runs his fingers through my hair, and I moan in delight. "I'm working on it. Thursday after work, just as you requested."

"Maybe I should just call in sick."

"Maybe you should keep that option open for Friday, just in case we have a late night."

"Hmm, good point, Mr. Jacobs. That's why you own your own business—because you use those big brains of yours."

Tris shakes his head. "You're pretty buzzed, but you're also adorable. Maybe someday you'll want to use your big brains and finally come join my company."

Tristan has asked me to be his CFO multiple times, but I've always worried about living *and* working together, and what it might do to our friendship. If we end up together long-term, it could be exhilarating to work side by side—

hello, afternoon delight meetings—but the added pressure could also be detrimental to our relationship.

"You're flashing that wrinkle again. Don't worry about it, Bex. I know you don't want to work for me."

"It's not that, and stop pointing out my flaws."

"Who says it's a flaw?" he asks seriously.

"Okay, my imperfections. Let's talk about work when I'm sober and after we've passed these dates, okay?"

"Anything you want, angel, but for the record, I like your imperfections."

I ignore how the latter part of that sentence makes me tingle all over. "Why do you call me that?"

His brow furrows. "You don't like it?"

"I love it, but I'm curious why you chose angel. And also . . . never mind." I turn away from him and try kicking off my shoes. I'm a bit unstable on my feet, and I trip.

Tristan's arm wraps around me from behind, and he pulls me flush against his body. "Careful, angel. Let's lie down, and I'll tell you a story."

Storytime in bed with Tristan? Yes, please.

We curl up together with my back to his front, and when I try to face him, he holds me in place. "Stay like this for this story, okay? It's a rough one."

I don't think I like the sound of that.

"The day we met was the best day I'd had in I don't know how long. No one knows this, but my mom had an affair, and my dad found out about it. They tried to keep it quiet, but whenever they thought I was asleep, they'd argue, yell, scream, and cry."

I already hate this story. "Tristan, I'm so sorry."

"It's okay. They're better than ever now, but it was hard back then. After a few months of hearing their private issues shouted through the house, I just couldn't take it anymore. I considered leaving home, but I didn't have any money or a place to go, and the thought of being homeless and potentially becoming addicted to drugs or ending up a prostitute wasn't my idea of getting relief."

He sucks in a deep breath and bile rises in my throat. I think I'm going to be sick because I know without a doubt where this story is going.

"Tris, you don't have to finish."

He places a lingering kiss against the back of my neck. "I want to, for many reasons. It got so bad one night. My mom was screaming she wished she never met my dad. The fifteen-year-old kid inside me took that to mean she wished I'd never been born. I was so messed up, Bex. I pulled out my laptop and started researching ways to kill myself."

Tears stream down my cheeks, and my heart feels like it's breaking. I don't ever want to imagine a world without Tristan. I clutch onto his arms tighter as he holds me.

"I'd finally decided carbon monoxide was the easiest way to do it. I was only waiting for the opportunity. My parents were going to therapy, and during their next appointment, I was going to use my dad's old Chevy to end my pain."

A sob escapes me, and he sighs against my skin. "Bexley, I'm sorry. I didn't mean to make you cry." He flips me around and brushes my tears away. "This story has a happy ending, you know."

The smile he gives me is genuine. It's Tristan's best smile, his happy one.

"That was the day I met you. The day you decided we needed to be friends. My troubles seemed so minor after that. You landed in my world, parted the clouds, and became my sun. You were my angel. You saved me, Bex."

My sniffles and sobs slow as he gazes into my eyes. I'm so in love with him, I can't even think straight.

"I'm not sure if I've ever had pet names for anyone before, but I don't think so. If anyone would have had one, it would've been Maria, and she hated them. One thing I do know is you're the only one I would've ever called angel—because that's what you are to me."

"What happened with your parents? Did you tell them?" I'm clutching him tighter than I should, but I need to feel him at this moment.

"That same night. They lost it, and we started going to family therapy. I think that's what brought them closer together actually. The idea of losing me because of their issues put things into a bigger perspective for them."

"I wish we'd known each other better back then so I could have helped you."

He chuckles. "Did you hear the story? You're the only reason I'm still here."

"What about Adam? Surely . . ."

He shakes his head vehemently. "No, only you. You're the only one I've ever told, aside from the therapist and my parents."

"And this is why you're so adamant about not cheating."

His face contorts into a scowl, and I reach out and caress his cheeks. "Cheating affects everything. I'm not sure how my dad forgave my mom, and I've never asked. I don't think I'd understand, and I wouldn't want to make him feel bad about himself. But yes, that's why cheating is a hard line for me. I'd never do it to anyone; I'd rather die first."

"No dying allowed. I need you too much." I pull his head toward mine, closing the gap between us, and his lips part as he lets me take control. We kiss slowly, deeply, and with more longing than I've ever felt. His hands roam my body. With each dip and curve they caress, he moans softly. I keep my fingers laced through his hair so I can hold him close. Losing myself in Tristan's love is what I was born for. It's a feeling I understand to the core of my being. I'm not complete without him, and I never have been.

When we break apart, he inhales deeply. I wonder if he's trying to suck in the essence of us as much as I am.

"Good night, Bexley. Sweet dreams." The longing in his voice matches how I feel right now.

"Tristan, stay, please."

He shakes his head, and his rejection hits me hard. "Not because I don't want to. If I stay tonight, we'll have sex." He points between the two of us. "Whatever this is between us—right now, I want to drown in it. I want to feel every one of your heartbeats against my chest. I want to be consumed by this connection in the most carnal of ways. I want to slip inside you, hold you down, and have you screaming my name so loudly that the neighbors bang on the walls. If I stay here tonight, I will *devour* you in every single way, and it still might not be enough."

Sweet baby Jesus, I may spontaneously combust.

"Okay." It's the only word I can manage to speak when all I want to do is ride him until we're both spent and satisfied.

"Two more dates, Bex. Please don't let me screw them up." He kisses me reverently, and my body erupts in goose bumps. Tristan stands, and I miss him already.

"You couldn't screw up if you tried. Night, Tris."

When the door closes behind him, I reach for my journal and sit up. I have to get this down before I pass out. Between the alcohol and all the emotions I'm feeling right now, I need the outlet.

The good parts:

My parents love you, and what's better is you love them too.

You told me your deepest secret. I'm not sure if you realize how much your trust means to me, but in case you're doubting your decision, I'll take it to my grave.

You refused to sleep with me, and then you told me why. I'm pretty sure if you'd kept talking, I would've come from your words alone.

You want to keep dating. With each date, I learn more about you and about myself. Unlike other men, you talk to me and treat me as an equal. Your feelings are never off-limits to me, and it's one of my favorite things about you.

You were jealous of Finn. I know that shouldn't be a good thing, but I hope it means you love me, and I'm not alone in this. BTW, jealous Tristan is hot as fuck. I know being jealous doesn't feel good, so I'm going to bottle up your expression for a really lonely day and bring out the memory for some naughty fun. I'll do my best never to make you feel that way again.

I was jealous of Maria. This is good because even though I already knew I was in deep, I now know how far my feelings reach.

The bad parts:

Tonight, there were a lot of bad things. Still, none of them even come close to something that would make me walk away from you or from us.

We ran into Finn, and you didn't take it well.

Maria called, and I didn't take it well. I know we talked about it, but I'm still not sure how I feel about her coming back to town. Well, maybe that's a lie: one thing I know for sure is that I'm jealous and really insecure. I probably shouldn't be, but I can't help it. She's gorgeous, sweet, and sexy, and you loved her and probably still do.

You tag-teamed me with my mom. That wasn't nice. But I forgive you because a man who gets along with my parents is the best kind of man there is.

I'm beginning to wonder if I'm obsessed with you. I think about you all the time. Everything I do, I wonder if you'd approve. If it would make you happy. How it would make you feel. I've never been in love—is this what it's like? Measuring your every move against someone else's happiness and morals? I can't imagine it's healthy, and I don't think I'd want to do that with anyone but you. Knowing I'm doing something that pleases you, or something that hurts you, is the best and the worst feeling in the world.

You confessed you were going to try to leave this world at one point. Tristan, regardless of what may or may not happen between us, please tell me if you ever get to that point again. A world without you—my best friend, the man I'm head over heels in love with—would not be a world I'd want to keep living in. The way we connect . . . I don't think you're only supposed to be mine for this lifetime. I think you're supposed to be mine in every lifetime.

After tonight, after your confession, my dating ritual seems ridiculous. Whatever happens next, this is the last round of dating roulette. Win or lose, this game ends with you, and I think that's the way it was always supposed to be.

Last, but not least, tonight I had a glimpse of what it would be like to lose you to someone else. It hurt more than I'd ever imagined. I'm scared, Tristan. If this thing between us ends, I don't know how to stay friends, but I suppose we'll always try to figure it out over pancakes at Rudy's on Saturday mornings.

Twelve

Tristan

"Let me get this straight. Bexley is in her room right now getting ready to go out with another guy. And you're okay with this?" Adam's outrage proves my best friend has my back.

"Far from okay, but I trust her. She's not my girlfriend, and I can't tell her to fuck up her job. She promised her boss, and now she's stuck."

Adam's player dies on the screen, and he flops back against the couch. "This is fucked up, Tris."

"What's fucked up?" Bexley emerges from her room wearing my favorite dress. It's navy blue and hugs all her curves. She walks in front of me and crouches down, pulling her heels out from under the table. Her ass is molded to that dress and brushing against my calf. I don't even bother stifling the moan.

"Bex, you're killing him. Go change. You shouldn't be dressing that sexy for a co-worker. Go take Tristan's favorite dress off and put something else on."

Oh, hell. Adam said what I would have loved to, but I'm not a misogynistic asshole. I can't tell her how to dress, and even if I could, what she wears is not indicative of what might happen tonight.

After slipping her shoes on, she rises to her full height, nostrils flaring. "I'm going to pretend you didn't just say that to me. Tristan, can I see you in my room for a moment?" Bex stalks off.

"Great, thanks for that. I'll be back after she hands my ass back to me." Adam's laughter follows me down the hall. I step into the room while admiring the view of her backside. *Damn that dress.*

"Close the door," she calls out as she digs through her closet. Not only do I close the door, but I lock it too.

"I'm sorry. You know how Adam can be."

She ignores me as she flips through her clothes. "Is this your favorite dress?"

I walk toward her and pull her back to my front, letting my dick do all the talking. "What do you think?" I slide my hands up the front of her body and ghost them over her breasts.

"I think it's sad that Adam knows you have a favorite thing that I wear and I don't."

"Well, to be fair, it wouldn't have been gentlemanly or best-friend-like to say, 'Bexley, every time you wear that dress, my cock reminds me how much I love how you look in it.' But now that we're talking about it, you have no idea the number of depraved thoughts I've had about you in this dress."

"Fuck," she hisses as she kicks off her heels. "I'm running completely behind schedule. Unzip my dress and get out."

"You don't have to change, Bex. It's okay."

"Nope, it's not. I'm wearing the funeral dress. Attractive but low-key. I'm not changing for you, exactly . . . I'm changing for me. I don't want your favorite dress tainted forever, and if it affects you like this, it might affect Finn like that too, and that's not what I want."

"God I—" Can't believe I almost slipped and said I love you. Time to cover. "Wish you weren't going out tonight so we could have date number six." Also, true.

She turns her head and kisses me on the cheek. "Me too, and the quicker you unzip me, the faster I can get dressed, and the sooner I'll be home so you can kiss me good night."

I unzip her dress like I've done a thousand times before, but this time, I wish it was because we were about to slip between the sheets. When I reach the door, I pause with my hand on the doorknob. "Angel?"

"Yeah?"

"Try not to let him steal your heart, okay?"

She sucks in an audible breath, but I'm still not looking her way. "Never. It already belongs to someone else."

I let myself out of her room and lean against the hallway wall. My pulse thrums against my eardrum. I'm going to hate myself for not seizing that moment, but if I had, she would've never left the house tonight, and I can't be the reason she loses her job.

Adam and I resume our game, and within a couple of minutes, the doorbell rings.

"I'll get it," Adam says, jumping up. He knows it's Finn, and right now, it's a good thing to keep some distance between him and me.

"I'm here to pick up Bexley."

I don't even need to see his face to know he's wearing that same smug grin he had at the grocery store.

"And you are?" Adam crosses his arms in front of him. He could be a bodyguard with his physique, but Finn isn't riled in the slightest.

"Her date, Finn."

"My co-worker," Bex corrects, entering the room. Irritation flares in her eyes as she makes her way to me. Bexley leans down and kisses me right on the lips in front of them both. "I won't be home too late. Wait up?"

"Always." I make sure my reply is loud and clear.

Adam flashes Finn a smug grin, and the guy looks like he's sucked on a lemon. Serves the asshole right.

"Later, Bex," Adam says, closing the door behind them. "Dude, she really doesn't like that guy, does she?"

"*I* really don't like that guy. He said that to get a rise out of me. I know it."

Adam grabs a couple of beers and uncaps them before bringing me one. "Have you two fucked yet?"

"You know Bex doesn't have sex with her dates."

He eyes me skeptically. "All right, maybe you haven't had 'actual' sex, but admit it: you've seen her 'O' face."

I'm too frustrated to keep playing and toss down the controller. "Why do you ask? This is Bexley, not some random chick. I'm not giving you details, Adam."

He holds his hand up in surrender. "And I'm not asking for details. The way she stalked toward you and kissed you in front of us both was very un-Bex like. That wasn't a friends kiss, that was a he's-fucking-my-brains-out kiss. She just drew a definitive line in the sand with him. Why aren't you happy?"

"Did you see him?"

Adam shrugs. "He was a good-looking guy." When I narrow my gaze at him, he pounds the rest of his beer. "What? I can appreciate a good-looking man, and I'm secure enough in my masculinity to admit when I see one. You're pretty hot yourself, Tris, but that doesn't mean I want to fuck. I happen to love pussy, and that won't ever change."

There's the Adam I know.

I try to explain where I'm coming from. "He's smooth, sophisticated, and the typical Bexley date. But he's also sleazy. Saying he's her date, knowing damn well he isn't? That pisses me off."

Adam side-eyes me. "Calm down. First of all, you nailed it in a nutshell. Typical Bexley date. Those haven't worked out so well for her in the past ten years, have they? Secondly, it's obvious she sees through him and doesn't appreciate his tactics. Bex can handle him. Relax."

Adam leaves about an hour later, and I can't stop thinking about my parents. I never asked for details about my mom's affair, but I'll never forget one specific night when it all first came out.

It was a warm summer night, and all the windows were open. My parents were fighting again, and I was lying on my bed with the lights out. The covered patio was just to the right of my bedroom window, and my dad was out there smoking a cigar.

"Why him?" Dad's raspy voice carried easily through the still night. He sounded so choked up I could almost picture the tears streaming down his face.

The metal patio chair screeched across the cement. Mom's sobs followed the sound. "He made me feel wanted, desired."

"And I don't?" Dad was getting angry.

"Oh, honey, you do. No matter how hard I try to explain it, I'll never do it justice. He has an air about him. Assurance, confidence . . ."

"It's because he's a rich son-of-a-bitch. He can buy anything, including my wife, apparently."

The sound of her skin against his ricocheted into the night. "Hal, I'm so sorry!" she cried out, sobbing even louder. I couldn't believe she hit him.

"I shouldn't have said that. I'm sorry. I need to know, Nancy, please . . ."

My dad was broken; I could hear it in his voice. I was just as angry with my mom as he was. I no longer felt guilty for listening to their private conversation. My guilt for violating their privacy fell to the wayside, and I listened eagerly, hoping to understand why she did this to our family.

"It's a look he gets. He reaches out and touches my arm, and desire flares in his eyes. My heart races, and it becomes impossible to deny our chemistry. When I tried to assert myself and remind us both I was a married woman, he would compliment me. Remind me I have needs and that I'm more than a wife and a mother. It was like he could take away all of my worries and all of my fears. It was nice *to hand them over, to let him make me forget. I knew it was wrong, but when I would come home, I would feel closer to you."*

Dad snorted loudly.

Mom sighed.

"I know how it sounds, and I can't explain it at all, but it's true. Your jokes seemed funnier; your touch gave me butterflies again. Sitting with you and holding your hand made me happier than it had in years. Suddenly, I cherished you in a way I hadn't before, and I realized how much I'd neglected you, neglected us. I miss us, Hal, and I'm sorry for breaking our marriage and letting someone so unworthy come between us."

Later on, I figured out who my mom had been with, and he was a lot like Finn. He was sleek and sophisticated, and would do whatever it took to get what he wanted. My mom isn't a stupid woman; she never was. Either she pulled one over on my dad to get him to take her back, or he was one of those men who knew how to find a woman's weakness and prey on it.

Bexley isn't stupid, but she is compassionate and eager to please everyone, which is why I'm here worried about her instead of on our sixth date—as I originally hoped we'd be.

"Tristan, wake up."

I blink rapidly and find Bex kneeling on the floor next to the couch. Her thumb traces my lip, and she smiles as my eyes focus.

"What time is it?" I ask groggily.

She scowls but quickly makes her expression neutral. "Late, almost midnight."

"Oh." *If you don't have something nice to say, don't say anything at all.*

"Please don't be mad at me." Her pleading tone hits me straight in the gut.

"I don't have the right to be mad at you."

She flinches, but maybe this is a case of the truth hurting. "We went to dinner, and then I was supposed to show him around and get him familiar with the area. Instead, his friend got him an exclusive invite to a new jazz club. I tried to leave, but he said he wanted to repay me for helping him out. Then my boss texted me to check in, and I felt obligated to stay."

"You don't have to explain anything to me." I move to sit up, but she places her hand over my heart.

"I know I don't, but it doesn't change the fact I would have rather been on date six with you. Tomorrow night, I have something special planned for us. Dress for fun, and be prepared to be wowed."

This time, her smile is contagious, and when she leans down to kiss me, I let her. She tastes like whiskey and cinnamon. While the combination is sexy as can be, it also means she really did have a shit night.

"Whiskey, Bex?" I sit up and pull her to her feet so I can walk her to her door.

"What can I say? I told you I'd have rather been here."

"We'll make up for the lost time tomorrow." I lean down and kiss her briefly. "Good night, Bexley."

"Night, Tris."

Today has been rough. I woke up late, put out one fire after another at the office, and had to deal with my mom's wrath because she bumped into Bex's mom at the store, who raved about what a cute couple we are. Mom was hurt I hadn't told her and didn't believe me when I said there wasn't much to tell yet.

It's not like I can tell her there is a man in Bex's life who reminds me of the one she had an affair with. This entire situation has me on edge, and I can't shake it. I wish Bex would come work for me, but she loves her job.

By the time I finally drag myself into the house, I'm exhausted, but as soon as I see Bexley waiting for me, my mood lightens. It's date night, and once we get past Thursday, maybe it will be easier to let the Finn stuff go. If only she didn't have one more night to spend showing him the town tomorrow.

Her eyes are glimmering in excitement. "Are you ready?"

"Let me shower, and then we can go."

"Nope, trust me, you can shower when we get home. Change into something more comfortable, though."

I'm in a suit today, which is rare, but I had back-to-back licensing meetings and had to look the part of business owner instead of gamer.

By the time I make it back to the living room, Bex has her keys in hand and is bouncing up and down on the tips of her toes.

She squeals when she sees I'm ready. "I'm so excited; let's go!"

I follow her outside, laughing as we walk to the car. Her excitement is contagious. "Where are we going?" I ask.

"It's a surprise, but you're going to love it."

Bexley navigates the traffic like a typical LA native, and thirty minutes later, she pulls up behind an industrial complex in the valley. Once we're out of the car, she grabs my hand and pulls me to an unmarked door and knocks.

A college-age kid opens it and eyes her appreciatively. "You must be Bexley."

"The one and only, and this is Tristan."

"'Sup man, come on in. So, like I told you on the phone, the place is yours for the next three hours. Everything has been set to free play. I'll be at the desk if you need me or have any questions."

D. Kelly

The kid opens another door and ushers us into a huge open space. We're at a ticket counter filled with prizes, and when I look around, my eyes widen. Electronic games of all makes fill the space. I crane my neck to look up, and the second floor looks to be more of the same. Multicolored lights flash around the room as music and electronic voices from the games beckon my soul—I'm like a kid in a candy store. Bexley slides her arm through mine. "What do you think?"

I pull her close and cover her lips with mine. Our kiss is brief; I pull back a second after our tongues meet. I don't want to give the kid a show or start something I won't want to stop.

I'm blown away. "This might be the best date ever. You're amazing."

She shrugs. "I try. Come on, let's start with Skee-Ball."

As we walk farther into the warehouse, I'm able to fully comprehend what's here. This entire warehouse is an arcade filled with every game imaginable. There are pinball machines galore—a plethora from the seventies, eighties, and nineties. I can't believe she planned our date in this massive, two-story electronic paradise. I spin in a circle, trying to take it all in, and she laughs.

"Tris, reel in the inner geek and focus. There is so much to do, and we only have three hours to do it. Let's have some fun."

We spend the next three hours reliving our teen years and respective childhoods. We have dance battles even though we both suck. We shoot hoops, drive virtual race cars, have pinball tournaments, Skee-Ball competitions, play air hockey, and rotate through a plethora of video games. It's the most fun I've ever had on a date and the best company too.

When our time is up, we're both starving and exhilarated. We walk hand in hand to the car, and when we get there, I push her up against it. Our lips meet, and our tongues battle for power. She moans, and my dick jumps. Her sighs are the best aphrodisiac.

"Thank you for tonight. Hands down the best date ever. Can I buy you dinner?" I ask as we part. It's the least I can do after she went all out.

"You're welcome. I had a lot of fun too, but the best part was seeing the stress melt off you. You looked like you had a rough day today."

"I did, but it's nothing I can't handle. So dinner?"

She yawns and squeezes my hand. "I'm starving, but can we go home and get pizza?"

"Yup, that sounds good."

When we get home, Bex hops in the shower, and I get the plates and napkins ready for pizza night with a couple of bottles of water.

Thankfully, it's a different delivery driver than last time, and the timing is perfect. Minutes after the driver leaves, Bexley joins me, looking relaxed and comfortable in her pajamas.

"Mm, this is heaven." She moans as she takes a bite of her pizza. I wonder if there will ever be a time I don't associate her food appreciation noises with sex because now that I know what she sounds like when she comes, I can't unhear it.

I settle in with my pizza, and I see her eyebrow wrinkle begin to form. "What has you breaking in your wrinkle?"

She rolls her eyes but sets her plate in her lap. "What happened today? I haven't seen you so stressed out in a long time."

"Licensing issues with some upcoming games, production issues with the one that's releasing in the spring, and my CFO finally quit."

"Can I help? Maybe on the weekend I can come in and take care of the important stuff until you find someone new."

I finish my pizza and grab another piece. "Thanks, but it's not your job. I'll figure it out."

"Tris, I know it isn't my job, but I know the job. I helped you in the beginning, and I can help again. Let me do this for you, please."

She hasn't worked in my office before. Maybe if I let her, she'll realize she likes the environment and want to come work there. Wishful thinking, but with the end of the year coming, it could take a while to find someone, and I could really use her help.

"Okay, we can go into the office on Sunday for a bit, and you can help me sort through a few things. Maybe help me go through some resumes?"

"You posted the job already?" She sounds surprised.

"I had to; it's priority number one right now. Besides, as much as I'd love for you to take the job, I know you're happy where you are."

"Sometimes, I wish I wasn't." Her words are so soft they're almost a whisper.

"Why? I thought you loved your job."

"I do, but I hate seeing you in a lurch, and I know that if I were the one running your finances, you'd never be in one."

I put the plate down and reach for her feet, pulling them into my lap. Her eyes roll back in her head when I start massaging them. I try to ignore her soft sighs and focus. "I love you for wanting to help, but my problems aren't yours."

"There will never be a time when your problems don't affect me. I'm always going to be your best friend, and I'm always going to want what is best for you." Bex finishes her pizza and sighs blissfully. "I could get used to this."

I would rub down every inch of her body each night if she wanted me to. I'm starting to feel a little pushy about us, though, so I change the subject. "Where are you and Finn going tomorrow?"

"Don't say it like that. It's not a date, Tris, and honestly, I'm not sure. My plan is to show him a couple of gyms, popular neighborhood restaurants, and some places he can hang out and get a drink on the weekend or after work. I'm hoping if we drive around and I point them out, we'll be done in less than an hour. We're leaving straight from work."

I pull her up, and we start putting the food and dishes away.

She bends over to load the dishwasher, and I admire the view. "Well, if that's all you're doing, call me when you get home. Adam and I are going to find a bar and play some darts or pool. Maybe you can meet us if you're up for it."

"That sounds like fun. A night of beer, games, and two of my best friends is exactly what I need."

When I walk her to her bedroom, I pull her into a hug. For some reason, tonight I just want to have her in my arms.

Thirteen

Bexley

Sixth date notes

The good parts:

Tris, the look on your face when we walked into the arcade was worth every penny. You've been so stressed out lately, and when it all melted away from your shoulders, when your frown lines turned into smiles, it made me feel like the luckiest woman in the world.

At the arcade, it dawned on me how well we know each other. We didn't have to make awkward small talk, and we played off each other's cues. I already know what you love and what you don't. Dating you is like falling into a romance novel. Everything about us works, but I know even if we stumble, our love is stronger than our faults, and we'll always be okay.

Do you realize you leave your socks under the coffee table? That you rarely rinse your coffee mug? You always leave your wet towel on the bathroom counter and the lid off the toothpaste. You make this God-awful sound when you chug water after your run, and sometimes you snore loud enough to rattle the windows.

You're probably wondering how this is good. Your annoying habits don't bother me. They're practically endearing . . . okay, maybe not, but I'm used to them. I rinse your mug, I recap the toothpaste, I toss your towel in the hamper, your socks in your room, and when you snore, I pop in some earplugs. And when you chug your water, I watch as the sweat trails down your chest, across your abs, and down your happy trail. Feel free to chug away whenever you'd like as long as I get to enjoy the view.

You offered me a job again, and I know it's not only because we're friends, it's because you feel I'm the best person for your company.

You massaged my feet like it was no big deal. Feet are gross, Tris, but you don't seem to mind. At least they were clean this time.

The bad parts:

Not being able to tell you I love you yet. With each passing day, I want to confess. I want to whisper it in your ear, trace the words onto your skin with my tongue, and show you with my body. The wait is torturous, but you're worth the pain.

Watching you stress out about work. Do you know how much I want to throw caution to the wind and quit my job? It would be too much, too fast, and if we're going to be lovers and roommates, we need some distance so we don't tire of each other—although I can't ever imagine getting sick of you.

I had to turn the job down again. It kills me every time.

But the worst is that I'm sensing you pull away. I think you're scared I'm going to call it quits. I wish I could reassure you that's not the case, but I know you need to see it through to the end before you believe it. Don't pull away from me, Tris. I'm right here.

"The big date with Tristan is tomorrow, right? Number seven. Are you excited?"

Rita and I are eating lunch in my office with the blinds closed. I usually keep them open, but Finn's office is across the hall, and he's constantly looking over here.

"I'll be more excited after I finish showing Finn around tonight and can finally breathe."

Rita packs her salad container back in her bag and pulls out some grapes. "How is that going anyway?"

"He's a lot to handle."

She laughs. "He looks like it, in more ways than one."

Exhaling, I lean back in my seat. "Tristan doesn't like him, doesn't trust him, and he's right not to. Finn isn't taking the hint that I'm involved. He keeps pressing with inappropriate questions. I've dodged some of them, but then I thought maybe if I answered some, he'd let it go. He didn't."

"What's Tristan say?"

"Are you kidding? I'm not telling him that now. He'd have a fit about me going tonight, and I have to. I went to breakfast this morning with Bradley."

Rita's head snaps up, "Wait, Bradley, who you went to dinner with a couple of weeks ago?"

"The one and the same. We've been talking here and there; he's a nice guy. He wants to be friends, and he's going about it in a way that reminds me of how Tristan and I became friends. I think I have a soft spot for him," I say. Rita raises a brow but doesn't say a word. "Anyway, I told him about Finn, and he didn't like it either. He offered to run a background check on him for me."

"I hope you took him up on it."

"No. If he still pushes after tonight, I might, but maybe he's lonely and harmless."

She eyes me skeptically. "Why don't I call you once an hour tonight?"

"That would be great. I'm hoping I'll only be with him for an hour."

Rita gathers her things and stands. "Make sure you answer. If you don't, I'm going straight to Adam and Tris."

"Deal."

At six p.m. sharp, there's a knock on my office door.

"Come in." I look up from my computer, and Finn walks in. He leaves the door open and takes a seat.

He clears his throat. "I think I owe you an apology."

"For . . .?"

"Well, I was talking to my sister this afternoon and told her how you'd been showing me around, and how you seemed hesitant to talk about yourself. She asked for some examples and then proceeded to point out that you probably think I'm an overbearing creep."

"Maybe a bit," I reply with a slight grin.

"Right, so in the spirit of full disclosure, I'm recently out of a relationship. I jumped at the chance of relocation because of it. Meeting you at the conference seemed fortuitous. What were the odds you'd be from my new office? And the one assigned to show me the ropes?"

It's nice to see him relaxed and not trying too hard. "I understand, and it's okay. As long as we're clear that we can only have a working relationship. Tristan is important to me, and no one is going to come between us."

"We're clear. Here's what I'm thinking for tonight: show me all the must-see places, and then let me take you for dinner and a drink at this bar closer to our houses. Just as friends, I swear. It can be quick, but the thought of eating another dinner alone sucks, and as much as I love my dog, he doesn't talk back."

If we make it quick, I can still meet up with Tris and Adam. I can tell Finn is trying, and he feels bad. "Okay, but I do have plans later, so it will have to be quick. Let's get going."

We drove around for about forty-five minutes while I showed Finn some important places to know both close to work and close to home. He typed in names on his phone of places he was curious about.

The bar he directs me to is Just an Illusion. It's packed tonight already. "This is a little off the beaten path for you. How did you find it?" I ask, pulling into the parking lot.

"I was running and decided to see what was back here. The murals on the exterior piqued my interest, so I took a photo and looked it up when I got home. Have you been here before?"

I park the car and grab my purse. "Yeah, it's actually one of our favorite places. You know the band Bastards and Dangerous? Their cousin owns it, and they come here frequently. They have good bands that play here too. Also, their nachos are seriously to die for."

"Well, let's go have some. You can't go wrong with nachos and margaritas for dinner."

It's packed for a Wednesday, but it doesn't surprise me. As we weave our way through the cars in the lot, I remind myself to call Tris once we're settled.

Once we're inside, Finn puts his hand on my back and guides me through the crowds to the bar on the right-hand side. Just an Illusion has two, and I always go to the one on the left. I'm actually not sure if I've ever been to the other one, but there's a first time for everything.

We manage to snag two seats in the middle of the bar. It's so weird being here with someone else.

"Hey Bex, long time, no see! Who's the stud?"

Finn scopes out the pretty girl and flashes her an enigmatic smile. "I'm Finn, and you are?"

Sasha holds up a finger and turns her attention to me. "New love interest? Fuck buddy?"

I laugh and shake my head. "Actually, I'm seeing someone else. You're good."

Sasha leans forward, putting her cleavage on display, and immodestly holds out her hand. "Sasha, bar manager and bartender extraordinaire. Also, single and a freak in the sheets, in case you were wondering."

"Pleasure to meet you, Sasha, freak in the sheets. Is that a self-designated title or one you've earned?"

She leans in closer. "Both. If you're lucky, I'll show you sometime, and you can tell me if it's well deserved. If you're brave enough that is . . ."

The owner of the bar joins her and tries reeling her in. They're best friends, so he only half means it when he scolds her. "Sasha, less talking, more working."

Sasha flips him off but straightens up. "Ignore Jordan; he needs to get laid. What can I get you guys tonight?"

"Two orders of nachos—"

Sasha's eyes widen.

"One," I correct. "Finn, they're massive. If you're still hungry after, we can get more, but I don't think you will be."

"Okay, one order of nachos, and I'll take a margarita on the rocks."

"And I'll have a blackberry margarita, blended with sugar, no salt."

"You got it. I'll be back soon. Don't go anywhere, sexy. I'm not done with you." Sasha trails her fingers over Finn's hand, and he nods.

When she leaves, he scoots in closer to me and tilts his head against mine. It's so loud in here; it makes it much easier to hear him this way. "Is she always this forward?"

"Pretty much. Sasha is a woman who knows what she wants, and it seems like you've piqued her interest." I take a hit to the back, and I reach out for Finn's shoulder to steady myself.

"Sorry," the man behind me says sincerely. "I'm blocked in on the other side and was trying to squeeze out. This place is a madhouse tonight."

"At least he apologized." Finn reaches for my hand and holds on until I'm a little more stable on my stool.

"Thanks. You never know what you're going to get with people out drinking. Oh, and speaking of, I need to call Tristan."

I reach into my purse and pull out my phone, which is completely dead. Shit. I wonder if Rita has tried to call yet. I texted her right before we left the office and didn't even notice my power was low.

"Everything okay?" The bar is becoming increasingly louder as the band for the night sets up.

"My phone died."

Finn pulls his from his pocket. "Want to use mine?"

I consider it for a moment, but if I call Tristan from Finn's phone, they'll have each other's numbers, and with everything that happened the other day, I don't think that's a good idea. Finn's done a complete one-eighty tonight, and if he and Tris hadn't gotten off to such a rocky start, they could possibly be friends. I would call Rita, but she switches her number like underwear, and I gave up trying to memorize them long ago.

"Nah, it's okay. He knows I'm out tonight. I was just going to update him on where I am."

"Don't take this the wrong way, and feel free to tell me it's none of my business, but is he a bit overprotective?"

Sasha picks the perfect moment to drop off our drinks. "I'll be back in a few with your nachos. Sorry for the wait, but the kitchen is slammed tonight. Next drink is on the house!"

I look up at her and shake my head. "Thanks, but I'm only having one tonight."

Sasha isn't having any excuses. "No one turns down a free drink in my bar. I'll get you an Uber if I need to. Live a little, Bex." She leans in close and licks her lips as if she's going to kiss me. Finn takes in the two of us like a man who's found his favorite porn. "Eli Watts is going to play in a bit. Shh, don't tell anyone." Sasha winks at me and kisses me on the cheek before moving to another customer.

Finn clears his throat. "Is she always like that?"

I gulp down half of my drink and fan my face with a napkin. "I'd have to say that's a first. I think she's trying to get your attention."

He laughs. "She's definitely got it. So, about my earlier question . . . too much?"

Damn, I thought I dodged a bullet. "Tristan is protective but not excessively. We've been through a lot together, and I'm equally protective of him. I'm not calling him because I have to. It's a mutual respect thing. We don't make each other needlessly worry. If we're going to be late, we call."

"Not text?"

I shake my head and finish off my drink. Sasha notices and tips her head toward me. I turn my attention back to Finn, "That's a me thing. Texting is impersonal, and with Tris . . ." As I push my glass away, I release a sigh. "I love his voice. It's the easiest way I can know what he's thinking or how he's feeling."

Sasha drops off a new round of drinks, and Finn raises a brow. "All from the sound of his voice? You know him that well?"

These margaritas are so good. I've chugged about a quarter of it before answering him. "Absolutely. There's a certain edge he gets to his tone if he's had a bad day. Or this sort of relaxed laziness to it if he's having a great day. When he gets sort of monotone, it means he's really not paying attention to me at all but in a developing zone."

"Developing zone?"

I nod and sip some more margarita. I'm feeling it already; they're stronger than usual tonight. "He owns a video game company. Tris is a genius. But when he's lonely, he gets this sad infliction in his voice, and that's my least favorite sound. Lately, though, since we've been dating, he has this new sort of huskiness, and I'm not exactly sure what it is, but I like it."

Thinking about Tristan puts a smile on my face, and I lean my head on Finn's shoulder. He wraps an arm around me like a good friend would do and speaks into my ear. "I'm pretty sure that voice means he's in love with you, and if I had to guess, I'd say the feeling is mutual. I also have a feeling you're already drunk, and that Uber Sasha promised is going to be our ticket home tonight."

Sasha grins as she places our nachos in front of us. I'm starving, so it's perfect timing. "Did I hook you up or what?"

I place my hands on the bar, and Finn covers one with his as I steady myself.

"You okay?" His concerned expression warms my heart.

"I'm great." I shove a nacho in my mouth with my free hand, and Sasha clicks her tongue.

"You're a lightweight, Bexley. I gave you one extra shot in each margarita and look at you. Better eat those nachos and tell me when you want that Uber." She laughs as she walks away.

Finn releases my hand as he digs in. "You're right; these nachos are amazing."

"Told you so. Damn, I'm drunk. If I call Tristan now, he'll want to come get me."

"Is that what you want?" Finn takes a sip of his drink.

"No. I think I want to go home and surprise him by crawling into his bed."

He chuckles. "That's the kind of girlfriend I need. Why don't you finish your drink, eat your nachos, and we'll stay and watch Eli. I'm only going to have the one drink so I can drive you home and catch a ride to my place from there."

"Yeah, that sounds like a perfect plan. It would be a shame to miss Eli; I had the biggest crush on him when I was a kid. Now he's all grown-up hotness."

Finn shakes his head when I gush about Eli. "I'm not sure I can attest to his level of hotness, but even the girls in my college were hung up on the guy."

"So how old are you?" I pop a chip in my mouth and wait for his answer.

"Thirty-two."

"Hmm, I'm pretty sure Sasha just turned thirty . . . I think."

"How old are you? Or do you subscribe to the mentality that a woman should never tell?"

Laughing, I shake my head. "I'm not old enough yet to have that mentality, but one day, I probably will. I'm twenty-six."

"You're mature for your age."

"Like you're so much older than me."

He finishes chewing his chip before responding — brownie points for that. I've been out with a decent number of guys who talk with their mouths full, and it's nasty. Finn's eyes meet mine. "I didn't mean it in a bad way. I've been out with younger women before where it's obvious how young they are. I thought you were older and looked damn good for your age."

"Well, thanks . . . I think."

Sasha pops by with two more drinks. Finn waves his off. "Sorry, since you got my ride wasted, I'm now the DD."

"And I'm already drunk, so I should probably sober up."

Sasha grins. "Girl, you've got a ride, and Eli is coming up. Might as well keep drinking while that sexy piece of ass croons his heart out. I'll bring you both some water, though."

She's back a few seconds later with two glasses of water and her phone number for Finn.

"Call me sometime if you want to figure out that answer for yourself. Fair warning: I'm a no-strings-attached kind of girl. Don't call if you're going to get all emotionally attached to me."

Some days, I swear Sasha is my hero.

By the time Finn walks me to my door and calls for his ride, it's close to midnight. He's about to put the key in the lock when the door swings open.

"Rita? What are you doing here?" I'm surprised to see her.

Her expression is neutral, and I can't figure out what is going on. "I've been calling you all night."

"My phone died."

"Her phone died." Finn's words land on top of mine, and for some reason, I find it hilarious.

"What he said," I tell her, and then laugh some more.

Rita groans as I stumble into the house. "Thanks for bringing her home, Finn, but I've got it from here."

"No problem. Have a good night, ladies. Thanks again, Bexley. I'm glad we worked things out."

"Me too. Night."

Rita closes the door, and I'm trying to kick off my shoes, but for some reason, one of them won't come off.

"Oh Bexley, what did you do?" She sounds sad, but until I get my shoe off, I can't hug her to make it better. Rita kneels and removes it for me.

"Sasha got me drunk. Free shots for Bex tonight, but she didn't know I was supposed to meet up with Tris. I've been dying to crawl into bed with him all night."

"Dammit, Bexley." Rita sighs. "I can't have this conversation with you while you're drunk. Come on, let me help you get ready for bed."

"Rita, you're sweet, but I think Tristan can do it. I'm so ready for these dates to be over. All I want to do is crawl between his sheets and call date seven a slumber party."

She rubs her face with her hands. "That's not possible. Tristan is spending the night with Adam."

"Oh." My expression falls, and it's obvious Rita feels sorry for me.

"How much did Sasha give you to drink?"

"Six or eight shots? I'm not sure; she was burying alcohol in my margaritas. But I had at least . . ." I tick off the drinks on my fingers. "Three or four? Four, all three of mine and the one Finn didn't drink I sucked down during Eli's set."

"Eli Watts?"

"Yes! I would have called you but"—I pull my phone from the front pocket of my jeans where Sasha tucked it as she helped me into the car—"phone is deader than dead."

Rita closes her eyes and exhales. "Why don't you let me charge that for you, and we'll talk in the morning. I'm not sure either of us is going to make it into work."

"Oh, we'll be fine."

Rita eyes me apprehensively but doesn't argue. She helps me change into my pajamas, and I can't stop yawning.

"Bedtime, drunkie," Rita encourages.

I'm starting to sober up a bit, which is probably why I'm so sleepy. "Why don't you sleep in my bed and I'll sleep in Tristan's room?"

She hesitates. "I'm not sure that's such a great idea."

"Sure, it is. Tristan won't care, and it will be nice to fall asleep with his scent surrounding me. Maybe if I'm lucky, he'll come home before work and wake me up."

Her eyes dart back and forth between my bed and me, and she gives in. "Okay, thanks. If you wake up before me, wake me up please."

"Yup. Thanks for helping me tonight. You're my best friend for a reason."

"Yeah, yeah, get some sleep."

Once I'm cuddled up in Tristan's bed and as comfortable as can be, Rita's sad face lingers in my mind. I'm a bad friend. It looks like she needs someone to talk to, and I'm useless tonight. Tomorrow, though, I'll help her figure out what's wrong.

D. Kelly

Fourteen

Tristan

12 Hours Earlier

This morning, I kissed Bex goodbye and promised her I'd give her a call later and tell her where Adam and I were going. I went to work, had a few meetings, and then left early to plan our seventh date tomorrow.

It hit me in the middle of the night what I wanted to do for her. It's so simple in theory, but making it happen is a different story.

When we were teenagers, if I'd have taken Bexley out for a first date, it would have been to Rudy's, simply because it's her favorite place. It's why that would have been my choice for our first date a few weeks ago, but the pick wasn't mine.

Now, I'm sitting in Rudy's cramped office in the back of the diner and hoping I can make some magic happen on short notice.

"What can I help you with, Tristan?"

The older gentleman sitting across from me still wears the same mischievous smile he did the first time we met. For a man in his late seventies, he's smart as a whip and involved in all the day-to-day business of the diner. Hell, he even cooks occasionally.

I straighten my shoulders. "I was hoping you could help me with an unusual request."

He leans back in his chair and steeples his fingers. "I'm listening."

"Bexley and I are dating, sort of."

"Is that what the youngsters call it these days?"

The old man actually makes me blush. "No, not like that." I take a few moments to explain Bex's odd dating habits. "Anyway, date seven is tomorrow, and although it's the last 'technical' date, it's also the start of a new beginning for us. At least, I hope it is."

"You know, when I met my Mary, God rest her soul, she had a lot of suitors, too. I'd been saving up money from working at my old man's diner so I could have a nest egg after high school." His eyes light up as he shares the memory. "One day, the carnival came to town, and she was looking at it from outside the fence with stars in her eyes. I couldn't run home fast enough to get my money. When I got back, she'd traveled along the fence, looking inside at all the attractions. I asked her if she'd like to go on a date with me inside the carnival." He picks up a photo and shows it to me. It's from their wedding day.

"This is a great picture. You both look very happy."

"That we were for fifty-five years. The carnival was our first date of many, and every year when it came to town, I always made sure to take her back and relive that first night."

I lean forward in my seat and pass his photo back. "Then maybe you can understand. Rudy's is Bexley's and my carnival. I'd like to rent it out tomorrow night. I'll pay you whatever you'd like, cover your costs. As long as you can have a waitress and someone here who can make chocolate chip pancakes, that's all we should need."

Rudy's eyes glass over, and he rubs his face. "My Mary's birthday is this Saturday. I think maybe this is her way of letting me know she's thinking of me too. What time do you want me to close?"

Rudy and I hash out the details, and I leave the diner feeling better than I have in months. It might not be a vacation, or an expensive night out on the town, but I think Bex will love it.

"Ready to go?" Adam shows up at the apartment right on time. It's six thirty, and I figured if we left a little later than we originally planned, Bex would get to spend most of the night with us. She and Finn got off about thirty minutes ago, so she should be almost done with him.

"Yup." I lock the house behind me and follow Adam to his car.

We decided on Just an Illusion so we could play some pool and get good food at the same time. Besides, Bexley loves it there, and Adam said Sasha is working tonight. She and Bex have a strange friendship. They don't talk outside of the bar, but they're great friends when they're at the bar at the same time.

"There is a rumor Eli Watts is playing here tonight," Adam says as he pulls into the parking lot.

"Well, that explains why it's so fucking crowded on a Wednesday."

Adam finds a spot, and we head inside. "You know, Bexley is going to want to stay all night. Eli is worth a sick day tomorrow for her."

I groan because it's Eli, and I'm not a fan. But thinking about how undeniably happy it will make Bex to see him play makes me smile.

"You're so fucking whipped it's not even funny." Adam laughs as he opens the door and heads upstairs toward the pool tables. We manage to score a table overlooking the far bar and the stage.

"Man, I'm just happy. This has been a long time coming. What about you and Rita? How's that going?"

One of the waitresses grabs our order real quick, and then Adam spills. "The sex is fantastic, and she's pretty cool. We're just seeing where it takes us."

"Uh-huh, and when are you supposed to meet up next?"

"She's going to talk to Bex about coming here with her tonight. She has to help her grandma with some stuff, so she might show up at my place later, depending on how long we're here."

The waitress brings our beers, and while Adam orders some appetizers, I scan the crowd below.

"Tris, what are you ... Holy fuck, is that Bex?" Adam leans forward. His disbelief mimics mine. Finn and Bex are walking through the crowd, and Finn has his hand on her lower back, leading her to the bar.

I bring my beer to my lips and watch as he helps her get seated. What are the fucking odds they're directly in my line of sight?

"I'll be right back," Adam says, but I barely hear him. I'm not sure how long he's gone because my eyes are drawn to Bex.

"Here, you're going to need something stronger than that tonight." Adam's back with a flight of five tequila shots. After slamming one back, I look at him to take the next one, but he slides the flight closer to me. "All yours, Tris. I'll nurse my beer for now."

Sasha's been chatting Finn and Bex up for a few minutes, and they all look pretty fucking cozy.

"For someone who couldn't wait to ditch this guy tonight, she sure looks like she's having fun."

Adam's gaze bounces between them and me. "Why don't you call her? Or better yet, go let her know you're here. She knew we were going out tonight; maybe she came to find us?"

I consider what he's saying, and I know I should give Bexley the benefit of the doubt. She's never done anything to make me question her. But when Finn rests his head against

133

hers, and she leans in closer and rubs up on his shoulder, I'm seeing red.

I slam down two more shots and then pick up my phone to call her. I watch as she pulls her phone from her purse, looks at it, touches the screen, and puts it back on the counter. It goes to voicemail, and my heart sinks in my chest.

"Son of a bitch," I snap, and Adam looks at me disbelievingly.

"Did she just really send you to voicemail?"

"Apparently so."

Unsure of what to do next, I take the last two shots and wait for the alcohol to kick in. After everything I told her about my parents, I can't believe she would do this to me. Especially with someone like Finn.

"Did Sasha just kiss Bex? Damn, that's kind of hot, Tris. Maybe you should go down there and get in on that action."

"Fuck that. I don't want any of that action right now. Maybe not ever again."

Adam sighs, and I watch as Bex guzzles her margarita. "Tristan, Bexley loves you. I'm not one to play devil's advocate, but I really think you should go talk to her. See what her reaction is when she sees you. I'll stay right here, and you can tell her we saw her from our table."

"Nope, not fucking doing it." The tequila is doing its job, and for right now, I'm content to wait and see.

We watch as the two of them drink and talk animatedly. Bexley seems excited about whatever she's talking about. "She's just as excited now with him as she was with me on our date last night."

"I'm sure she's just being . . . polite. Isn't this part of a favor she's doing for her boss?"

I snort and shake my head. "If I asked my employees to do these kinds of favors, I'm pretty sure I'd get sued."

Adam runs his hands through his hair and sighs. "You have a point."

A few minutes later, she's leaning onto his shoulder, and he has his arm around her. That's enough for me. "Let's go. I'm done here."

"Tristan, let's just wait a minute. Or better yet, let me go talk to her."

I shake my head and look back down. I have to grip the edge of the table to steady myself. They're fucking holding hands. Adam can't even cover his surprise—his wide-eyed expression says it all.

"I'm out of here. You can take me home or I can Uber."

As I storm out of the bar, I try to take some deep breaths, but with each inhale and exhale, my heart shatters even further. Once we're in the car and on the way to my place, the pain slams into me.

It's over. I've lost my best friend and the love of my life.

"What are you going to do?" Adam asks when he pulls into my complex.

"I'm going to pack a bag and go to a hotel for a few days. I need some time to think."

"Don't be ridiculous, Tris. You can stay with me."

I'm a few steps ahead of him as we walk inside. "Nah, I can't. That's going to be the first place she'll look. I can't talk to her right now. I need time to . . ."

"To what?"

"Figure out if I can ever look her in the eye again."

"Damn, go pack your stuff. I'm going to call Rita."

Once I'm inside my room with the doors closed, I have to blink back tears. How could I have been so fucking stupid to cross that line with her? I grab a duffle bag from my closet and pack enough stuff to make it through the weekend.

D. Kelly

Before grabbing my bathroom items, I reach for the notebook on the side of my bed and sit down to write Bexley a note. After I'm satisfied, I get my things from the bathroom and zip my bag.

The doorbell rings, and by the time I make it to the living room, Rita is kissing Adam. Fuck, they look happy. I wish I could say the same about myself. I clear my throat, and they separate.

Rita locks her solemn eyes on mine. "Tristan, I'm sure this is all just a big misunderstanding."

I know Rita means well, but I can't do this with her. "Nope, it was pretty obvious."

She shakes her head vehemently. "It doesn't make sense. We ate with the blinds closed today because he was creeping on her. We had a deal that I would call her once an hour, and if she didn't answer her phone, I would call you, and we would track her down. Once I got Adam's message saying she was at the bar, I didn't bother calling. Maybe I fucked up and should have. I'd just assumed if she were in trouble, you'd be the first one to take care of it."

With a shrug, I heave my bag over my shoulder. "I don't know what you want me to tell you. Whatever happened at lunch doesn't coincide with what happened at the bar. You're welcome to stay here and wait for her, but I'm out."

I head toward the door, needing to get out of this oppressive apartment. Everything in here reminds me of her. It smells like Bex, and instead of wanting to drown in the pleasureful aroma, I want to vomit.

Rita calls out after me, but I ignore her. "Wait! Could he have drugged her? Maybe we should call the bar and have them keep an eye on her."

"Sasha would have picked up on it if she were drugged. That woman has the drug-sensing abilities of a canine," Adam tells her before kissing her goodbye. "I'll call you when I get home."

The drive to the hotel is quiet. I booked a suite because if I'm going to be miserable, I can do it in a nice room with most of the comforts of home. Adam tried to come inside with me, but I told him to go back to Rita. All I want right now is to be alone.

After I've taken a hot shower and cried like a little bitch, I'm exhausted. It's after eleven, and Bexley hasn't tried to call me all night. She hasn't even texted, which would be rare for her, but she does it occasionally if it's important. I can't understand how I've become such an afterthought.

I've given consideration to Rita's suggestion about her being drugged, but she looked fine, and Adam was right: Sasha would have noticed, without a doubt. Plus, I might not like Finn, but he's a professional with a lot on the line. It's possible he could drug women, but unlikely for a guy like him. He's all about the chase.

I didn't think I would fall asleep, but my phone rings a little after twelve and wakes me. It's Adam.

"Hey." My voice is raspy, and I sit up and grab my water from the bedside table.

"Rita texted me a few minutes ago. Bexley is home, and she's extremely drunk."

"Good for her."

"Tris, I know you're a bit drunk yourself, so I'm not going to get into this with you too deep tonight, but Bex's phone was dead. Before she even got to the bar."

"No, that's bullshit. She pulled it out when I called."

He sighs. "I know, but you two have always had an eerie connection. Maybe she sensed you. Rita has the phone;

she plugged it in and even sent me a screenshot of when it powered up. The missed calls and messages were all there. She wasn't lying."

"And she couldn't have used Sasha's phone to call me? His phone? She couldn't have said, 'Hey Finn, I'm supposed to meet Tristan. We have plans.'"

"You're right, she could have, but she didn't. Rita said Bex's number-one goal when she got home was to crawl into your bed and beg you for a slumber party for date number seven."

I'm conflicted. On the one hand, that would have been incredibly sexy, and on the other, I know what I saw tonight, and her comfort level with Finn was beyond co-worker status. "I need time to think, Adam, and to get some sleep. I'll talk to you tomorrow."

I power off my phone and set it back on the nightstand. All I want to do right now is sleep and push Bex and Finn out of my mind.

Fifteen

Bexley

Sweet Jesus, why does my head feel like someone used it as a ping-pong ball all night?

"Rise and shine. We have major damages to fix, but first, you need to brush those teeth and drink the coffee I just made you."

"Rita?" I blink rapidly, trying to open my eyes, which are currently stuck together by sleep and the makeup I must've forgotten to wash off before bed. Gross.

"The one and only. Normally, I wouldn't wake you, but it's eleven a.m., and if we're going to use our sick days to play hooky, we better make the most of them."

I sit up quickly once her words have processed and regret it immediately. When I clutch my head in my hands, she snorts but has the decency to help.

Rita holds out the ibuprofen for me. "Take these and drink this water. Adam even dropped off a greasy bagel sandwich from your favorite hangover spot."

After tossing back the pills and drinking half the bottle of water, my eyes finally meet hers. As I look around, I realize I'm in Tristan's room, and last night starts coming back to me slowly.

"Why is Adam being nice to me?" I ask.

She gazes at me sympathetically. "Go wash your face and meet me in the kitchen. This is a long story."

The water sloshes around my stomach like the ocean during a storm, but I'm not sure it's only the hangover making me nauseous. I'm growing more and more uneasy by the minute. After I've washed my face, brushed my teeth, and relieved my bladder, I feel marginally human again.

By the time I join Rita in the kitchen, she has my coffee made just the way I like it and the sandwich heated and on a plate for me.

I flash her a weary smile. "Maybe I should marry you. Why are you spoiling me this morning? Should I be worried?"

She finishes making her coffee, and I bite into the sandwich. Nothing is better than an egg, cheese, and bacon bagel to soak up the bitter remnants of alcohol.

When Rita sits, she brings her mug to her lips and hums as the coffee hits her tongue. I take a few more bites and let her get the caffeine jumpstart she needs.

After pushing away the rest of the giant breakfast sandwich, I sip my coffee before bringing my eyes to hers. "Can you explain to me what in the world is going on?"

"Oh, honey, I wish I didn't have to. Let's take our coffee in the living room and get comfortable."

Once we're settled on the couch comfortably, my nerves kick in. "Rita, why do I feel like you're about to give me bad news?"

"Because I am, but before we talk about what happened last night, tell me what happened with you and Finn. How did we get from him being a creeper and me checking in on you, to you partying it up with him at the bar?"

I take a few minutes and fill her in about what happened in my office. "I enjoyed his company last night. He wasn't the total asshat he'd previously shown himself to be. We drove around, I showed him some must-know places, and we went to the bar. I pulled out my phone to call Tris, and it was dead. By then, Sasha was sabotaging my drinks with extra shots, but I didn't know it."

"Why didn't you use the bar phone or Finn's to call Tristan, or me for that matter?"

Damn, I feel like a jerk. "I'm sorry. I should have called you, but I couldn't remember your new number." I explain to her my debate about Finn and Tris having each other's numbers. "Finally, I shrugged it off and figured I'd be out of there in less than thirty minutes, and I'd see Tristan soon."

Her irritation fades as her eyes light up. "But instead you were wasted and stayed for Eli's show."

"You don't know Sasha, but she's hard to say no to. She just wanted me to have a fun time, and since she and Finn were flirting all night, and they exchanged numbers, I think she was trying to keep us around a bit longer. By the time the second drink arrived, I was really buzzed." I finish telling her everything I remember about last night, and she takes it all in, asking very few questions.

Rita tucks her feet beneath her and faces me on the couch. "Last night, Tristan and Adam were also at Just an Illusion. They were upstairs and had the perfect view of you and Finn sitting at the bar . . ."

When Rita finishes her story, I'm sick to my stomach. Tristan thinks I was flirting with Finn.

"That's not true, though. I would *never* do anything to hurt Tristan." *How could he possibly believe this?*

She reaches over and squeezes my hand as I blink back tears. "I know you wouldn't, and I think it's shitty they didn't tell you they were there. But I can also understand why they didn't. I know you would've never intentionally done anything wrong."

"Rita, I love him!"

"I'm sure you do, but he's hurting right now. Regardless of how you feel, he saw what he saw, and so did Adam."

My head is spinning. I have to figure out how to make this right. I recall my version of the night. The guy who bumped into me, all the gushing I did to Finn about Tris and how incredibly smart and dedicated he is to his business. I jump up from the couch, not willing to waste another minute.

"What are you doing?" Rita asks.

"Going to Adam's to talk to Tristan."

Rita stands and places her hands firmly on my shoulders. "First of all, you have to shower." When I start to argue, she cuts me off. "No one wants to smell last night's hangover lingering. Especially if there's a hint of Finn's scent on you."

Okay, she's got me there.

"Secondly, Tristan didn't go to Adam's; he rented a hotel somewhere. Before you ask, I don't know, and Adam wouldn't tell me where. You're going to have to get that information from him or get ahold of Tristan himself to figure that out. Bexley, it was all Tris could do not to cry in front of us last night. He was devastated. Honestly, I never took him for such an emotional guy who would jump to conclusions." She shrugs and continues, "but when you see something with your own eyes, even if it's out of context, I guess your feelings tend to take over."

When she releases me, I grasp onto the back of the couch. "This is about more than just me. His past is coming back to haunt him, and I'm the catalyst. You can go home if you want, or maybe go see Adam. I'm sure you two can take this opportunity to have some fun today."

"Are you sure? I'm more than willing to stay and help you figure this out."

I pull her into a hug and release her quickly, so she doesn't absorb my stench. "You're a good friend, but I need to figure this out on my own. I'll call you if I need anything. And if you hear anything I should know . . ."

"I'll call you."

Rita gathers her things and brings me my phone. "It's all charged and waiting for you."

"Thanks, and thanks for staying with me and believing me."

"Anytime, and Bex, I know emotions can get high, but try to remember that two people can see the same situation and come away with different interpretations, yet both still be correct. You may not feel like you did anything wrong, but Tristan still saw what he did, and his emotions about the situation are still valid."

"I'll try." I close the door behind her and check my phone. There's one missed call from Tristan and some texts from Adam. I can tell from his messages, last night was difficult for them both.

I take a deep breath and try to call Tristan. His phone goes straight to voicemail, and on the third attempt, I leave him a message. "Tristan, it's me. Please call me back. I'm so sorry about last night, but I promise you, it's not at all what you thought. I understand that you're angry and hurt, but please let me explain."

More than anything, I want to tell him I love him, but not now. Those words between us should be special—not something said to try to bridge the gap between us. He deserves better than that. We both do.

After I've showered and dressed, I call Adam as I gather my things.

"Bexley," he answers as per his usual fashion.

"Adam, please tell me where he is. I have to fix this."

"You know I can't do that, babe."

I sigh as I lock the door behind me. "Have you at least talked to him today?"

"No, his phone goes straight to voicemail. He was pretty wasted and upset last night; he's probably sleeping it off."

My heart leaps slightly. "Was he wasted before he saw me? Is there any chance he'll realize he's overreacting?"

"Hang on a second." The sound of a door closing meets my ears as I climb into my car. "Tristan had barely cracked a beer when you came in. It wasn't until he was ready to beat Finn to a pulp or storm out of the bar that I got him a flight of tequila shots."

"Oh, well, it's okay. I'm going to make him understand." My phone syncs to the Bluetooth as I turn my car on, and I'm able to put it down.

"Rita told me your side of the story. It's hard to believe based on what I saw last night, but if there's one thing I know, it's that you're not a liar. You know Tristan can be stubborn, but he'll come around eventually. After some time passes, I'll help."

My heart thumps rapidly against my chest. "Time? How much time, Adam?" I'm losing my shit, and I need to calm down. As I grip the steering wheel, I count to ten.

His answering tone sounds as defeated as I already feel. "I'm not sure, Bex. A few days, a few weeks maybe? I've never seen him so . . . crushed."

"Thanks, Adam. I'm going to try to find him, but I may be calling you back later. If he calls you, please tell him I'm sorry, and I want to make this right."

"Will do."

My car is practically on autopilot as I drive to Tristan's office. His isn't in the lot, but since he was drinking last night, it's probably at home. I sit parked for a few minutes and try to come up with a game plan.

I dig through my purse for my pass into his office. Once I have it firmly in my grasp, I steel my resolve and head inside the building. This building is like night and day, literally. The entire downstairs is a gamer's dream. It's basically three sections, one where there are desks, monitors, and computers, but the lighting is mostly done by the lamps on their desks.

Then there is an open gaming section with couches, chairs, game chairs, bean bags—whatever makes these guys comfortable while they're being creative.

The third section is more like individual soundproof offices where people can work or play if they prefer more of a silent and solitary environment. This area is Tristan's pride and joy. It's where all the magic happens, and anyone who comes into his office has to walk through here. At the end of the hall, I take the stairs up to the second floor. When I reach the top, it takes my breath away, just like it does every time.

Murals on every wall are filled with gamescapes—at least, that's what I call them. They're some of the most intricate scenes from Tristan's games. They rotate from happy to sad, light to dark, freedom to dungeon, but each of them contains a piece of Tristan for everyone to see. The pride I feel when I come here is so immense I don't even know how I keep it all inside.

It's brighter up here. The lights stay on, and this is where the executives work. The kitchen is always well stocked with snacks and drinks. Tristan wants all his staff members to be productive and happy, which is hard to do when you forget to eat or start feeling that afternoon sludge kick in. Most of the offerings are healthy, but he does have some treats too. Tristan loves his junk food as much as the next person.

By the time I make it to Tristan's office, it's obvious he isn't there. I've fielded quite a few people confused to see me here since he's out for the rest of the week. I suppose I'm not surprised, but I am disappointed.

I do take a moment to sit at his desk and leave him a note on the off chance he decides to pop in after hours. He keeps a photo of us next to his computer, and it brings a smile to my face. I'm trying hard not to let myself be sucked into the sadness. *This is only a misunderstanding.*

When I arrive back at the apartment, sadness settles over me with Tristan's abscence. I'd thought maybe he'd come home. I try calling him again, and once again, it goes straight to voicemail.

"Tristan, I understand you're hurting, but if you'd talk to me and let me explain I think it would go a long way toward fixing things. We've never fought before; can you believe that? Statistically, we were bound to have a fight eventually, but I hate feeling this way, and I can't imagine how you must be feeling. Can we fix this and go another ten years without fighting again? Call me . . . please."

Before I know it, I'm back in his room and notice a Post-it on top of his notebook next to his bed. I didn't see it this morning or last night, but I also wasn't paying much attention. It has my name on it, so I open the notebook, not at all prepared for what's inside.

Sixteen

Bexley

When I open the notebook, the lists he wanted me to keep from our dates make more sense because he's been keeping them too. Normally, I wouldn't read his thoughts without his permission, but he did put my name on the book for a reason.

Dating Roulette – First date

Bexley,

Since I asked you to keep track of my screw-ups and my non-screw-ups, I figured I'd try and give you my take on our dates too. Fair is fair, after all.

Tonight was our first date, but if you ask me, I think you got screwed. If I were going to take you on an actual first date, I probably would've taken you to Rudy's for chocolate chip pancakes. No, it's not the most romantic place in the world, but I know it's your absolute favorite. The thing is, when you came home drunk the other night and started talking to me in a way I never imagined I'd hear, it flipped a switch inside me.

After I put you to bed, I couldn't get you out of my mind. My dick was so hard, and I was conflicted. You're my best friend and getting off to visions of you was wrong, but Bexley, let me tell you something else—I've never felt anything so right in all my life.

147

As I stroked myself, I imagined it was you. Your name was on my lips when I came harder than I ever had before. Knowing I was going to ask to be part of your dating cycle had me just as excited as it did terrified. Never before have I allowed myself to envision a future for us, and suddenly, I can't picture a future without you.

That's how we ended up at Just an Illusion instead of Rudy's. There was so much I wanted to say to you, but I needed you to have a tiny bit of liquid courage so we could get through the discussion. For all your bravery with every other man in your life, you tend to hold back with me at times. It's a good thing; it means you care about what I think and how I'll respond. You let yourself be vulnerable with me, and I strive to never make you second-guess that choice.

One thing I'm not sorry about is our kiss. If for some reason we don't work out, that kiss will be the one I compare all other kisses to until the end of time. I'm hopeful what we needed was timing. Neither of us was ready before now for the tsunami of feelings headed our way. I'm ready now, Bex, and I hope you are too. There is no one I'd rather take the most exciting journey of my life with than you.

First date recap: *I've failed as far as giving you the memorable first date you deserve, but I'm hoping our first kiss knocks that failure down a few pegs. I can't tell you how excited I am for the next six dates and how much I hope I get to be the first who obtains the coveted eighth date and every date beyond.*

Wow, having insight into Tristan's heart and mind is a heady sensation. If the rest of these recaps give me as much hope as this one, I know the two of us will be fine.

Second date:
Bex,

Due to the fact we live together, some of these may run together a bit. I'm trying to jot things down as I think of them so that you have a full, comprehensive account of how I'm feeling through our dates.

We're about to leave on our second date, and I thought since we spent so much time together today, I would break this into a 'before date' and 'after date' summary.

Before: *This morning, I woke up excited. I've never felt like this before. It was better than any high I've gotten from my business successes. Better than college graduation, but similar to the day you decided we should be friends. That in itself should tell you something. I'm beginning to understand my feelings for you have been buried deep down inside of me for a long time. Last night when I realized it, I didn't sleep much and was awake with the sun. The only thing I wanted to do was crawl into your bed and kiss you. I wanted to know if we could replicate that magic again. Instead, I went and bought donuts, your favorites, made coffee, gorged myself while you got your beauty rest, and then went for a run to try and process all these new emotions.*

Just when I thought I had things under control, you asked for the boyfriend experience. Did I stop breathing when you said that? I feel like I lost control for a minute. The thought of you never having that ripped me to shreds, but knowing I was going to be the one to give it to you—fuck, Bex—I'm still hard from the constant loop running through my head of what we might do tonight.

I'm just going to apologize now for whatever I do wrong. This whole date is wrong in so many ways. You deserve better than skipping ahead, but I promise since we are, I'm going to make it the most memorable boyfriend experience you can have. Walking you to your door tonight is going to be hard. Or maybe that will just be me.

After: *I wanted you to write down the fucked-up shit I did on these dates, but today, I think that honor belongs to you. It wasn't intentional, and I was more than a willing participant, but it was a special kind of hell* *pretending to be your boyfriend tonight. Not being able to do everything a boyfriend would actually do wasn't easy, but coming home and retreating to our separate rooms was worse. If you were mine, you'd be wrapped in my arms right now as we made love. After the night we had, we would be making love. I'd show you exactly how much I worship every inch of your delectable body, and then in the middle of the night, I'd get you on your knees and spank you until you cried out how sorry you were for torturing me. Your pussy would be dripping because being controlled turns you on. As soon as I slipped inside you, your inner walls would clench around me, and you'd shatter while calling out my name and your undying love.*

The problem is, I'm not your boyfriend, Bex, and I've only got five more dates to make you realize I should be. It's the most terrified I've been in my entire life, and also, the most exhilarated.

Second date recap: *The boyfriend experience may go down as my favorite date. Even with my conflicted feelings, it was a night I'll never forget. Don't let this be for nothing, Bex. I need you to want to be the air I breathe, or else I may have to break my first ever promise to you. After tonight, I'm not sure I could go back to how things were before. I thought it would be easy, but that was before I knew . . . I'm already in love with you.*

Tears stream down my cheeks. There is so much to unpack here. *Tristan loves me.* I knew it because I've always felt it, but now it's here in black and white, and it should feel better than anything but how can it when we're in such a bad place? I want to be more than his air; I want to be his everything because he's already mine. But if we can't go back, what does that mean for us now when he won't even talk to me?

Non-date:
Bexley,

You're out of town, but our date is tomorrow. Adam came over tonight and asked me if I'd marry you. Typical random, out-of-the-blue Adam BS. It got me thinking, though, about you and me, and what we're doing.

We're taking a huge risk with our friendship, and I can't help but think that means something greater than either of us are considering. Would we have jumped into this if we weren't ready for more? After a night full of reflection, I can honestly tell you . . . I wouldn't have. My feelings for you have been growing for the last ten years. I know we're not there yet, not at that place in our relationship, or as the case may be, non-relationship since we're still working through these dates. But I wanted you to know that someday, when the time is right, I will absolutely marry you. In fact, there's nothing I'd like more.

After date seven, you have to make a choice. To keep seeing me or to move on and start seeing someone else. I'm hoping it will be to keep going, but maybe I'll have a better understanding of what you want after the third date. After all, that seems to be the defining date in most of your dating cycles.

How about I make you a promise?

Don't break my heart, and I will never *break yours.*

I'm sobbing so hard, I can't catch my breath. I'd marry you in a heartbeat, Tristan. It's you, and it always has been, but did I already mess it up? Did I break your heart last night? If I did, I have to figure out a way to piece it back together because your heart is the most precious thing in the world to me.

Third date:

Bexley,

As much as I missed you while you were gone, the way you kissed me when you came home today more than made up for it. That's what I keep trying to remind myself of when I think about you and Finn. I'm sure you'll be fine, but this is what I wanted to tell you today and couldn't.

Watch out for him, Bex. Some men can't handle being told no. Especially if they feel what they want is within their grasp.

Those men will try and get to know you and learn what they can about your significant other. Who knows, Finn may be a great guy and back off right away, but women like you are enticing. You're the whole package, Bex—intelligent, successful, driven, sexy, sweet—and that is a powerful combination.

You said you wanted to be mine. Remember that, Bex, for both our sakes.

Like most of your third dates, tonight was a game changer—at least for me. The way you opened yourself up and asked for what you wanted sexually blew my mind. It was positively cruel when you said you wanted me to take you bare tonight. You were testing me, pushing my buttons, but that's okay because I'm not going to waver. I've given in with certain things, but we're not going any further sexually until our last date.

I caught what you were saying tonight—you want forever with me—and I want that as well. We have all the time in the world, Bex, and I can't wait to share forever with you.

Third date recap: *We made it past the hump with flying colors. There are four more dates left, but you only get to pick the next three. Date seven will be my surprise.*

I wish instead of making notes we'd talked about how we were feeling to each other. Between his pages and mine, we're feeling many of the same things. Maybe if we hadn't focused so much on the dates being perfect and put that effort into communicating our feelings better, we wouldn't be in this mess we're in now.

Fourth date:
Bexley,
Today you showed your true nature. You compromised what you would've wanted for a date to make

me happy. I'm blown away by your kindness and will forever love you for it. Granted, I know it wasn't completely altruistic. You had your own motives, and being in my arms most of the night was the driving force. You should know that isn't the slightest hardship for me. If I had my choice, you'd be in my arms as often as possible.

I'd say there were three highlights of my night tonight: the first being the expression on your face when I bought you a funnel cake of your own. Sometimes it's as if you don't think I know you. I'd like to think I know you better than anyone else.

The second was carrying you in from the car. When I looked down at your sleeping face, I imagined seeing that same perfection each morning for the rest of my life. That's a future I'd love to be a part of.

The third was when you stumbled over your words and asked me to sleep with you. I knew what you were getting at, and I had no intention of letting you sleep alone after spending Halloween in a theme park geared to instill fear. You can barely watch a suspenseful movie without needing someone to hold your hand. It won't be easy, but it will be my absolute pleasure to be what helps you through the night.

Fourth date recap: *Perfection in every way. Three left to go until you're mine. Or until I'm yours, but if you want the truth—I already am.*

All the feels! I can't turn the page fast enough. Maybe there's a clue somewhere about where he is.

Fifth date:
Before:
Bexley,
For the first time since we started our dates, I'm having doubts. I can't tell if you're even aware that you were flirting with Finn, but I'm choosing to believe it's a subconscious thing. I don't think you'd ever hurt me intentionally, but you did.

Why couldn't you tell him I was the guy you're dating? I'm not sure you've ever hurt my feelings before, but today, for the first time, you did.

After:

This day was emotional. Everything I felt earlier about Finn got flipped upside down when Maria called. I'm pretty sure we've worked everything out now, but if there are any lingering doubts in your mind, I'm sorry.

I never wanted you to know that I almost killed myself. I can't stand the thought of you feeling sorry for me or seeing me as weak. It was a long time ago, and I was a mixed-up kid filled with fear and anxiety, resentment and pain. The only reason I told you, aside from it having to do with your nickname, is because Maria called.

Bex, moving with Maria was never an option. I loved her in my own way, and I was sad when she left. Losing someone and missing them is hard, but relationships end. Had it been you who had moved across the country for a job, I would've packed right along with you and relocated my company. What does that tell you?

Never doubt my love for you, Bexley; it's the one thing in my entire life that I know without a doubt I got right.

Tuesday is date number six; we're getting closer. I can't wait to see what you have planned for us.

At the end of each date, it feels like I can exhale. Can you tell how nervous I am? You've banished guys for much less than an ex trying to get back together. On the one hand, you know me better than anyone. You of all people should know my quirks inside and out, and I'm probably worrying needlessly. But on the other hand, we've never shared our intimate sides. What if I kiss funny? Use too much tongue, or forget to pop a mint?

There are only two more dates left, and then hopefully, these ridiculous thoughts will be out of my mind for good. Unless you break my heart.

Bexley, please don't do that.

Fifth date recap:
I feel closer to you than I ever have. It's terrifying in the best kind of way. If I can get past your outings with Finn this week and you can stop worrying about Maria, I think we'll be fine.

Oh Tristan, I'm so very sorry.

Sixth date:
Bexley,

Tonight was the best date ever. Well, it's tied with the boyfriend experience but for completely different reasons. You completely topped the amusement park on Halloween. I love that we can be ourselves and enjoy each other without all the difficult aspects of a date. The best part was seeing the excitement on your face when you realized how much I loved the arcade. That feeling of being happy because you made someone else happy is heady, isn't it? And knowing that's how you felt lured me into a false sense of security that you feel the same way about me as I do about you. I want to believe you do, you've shown me in many ways, but with date seven lingering over our heads, I'm afraid to trust it yet.

In the beginning, our dates were supposed to be about you, but lately, they've been about me. Why is that? I'm supposed to be the one giving you experiences. The goal was for me to give you all the dates you ever wanted so I could make you realize we're the perfect match. What happened, instead, is that with each passing date, I'm falling deeper in love with my best friend.

I still haven't figured out what I'm going to do for our seventh date on Thursday. I wish we could fly to Hawaii and spend a long, relaxing weekend alone. Instead, I need to think on a smaller scale because this isn't the ideal time of year for either of us to take a break from work. I'll figure it out soon, and hopefully, you'll love it.

Thank you for knowing exactly what I needed tonight. Once again, you've shown me why we're a perfect match. If only I could get rid of this lingering anxiety about us. When I hugged you good night, I didn't want to let you go. I've got a niggling fear that we won't make it through date seven, and nothing has ever scared me more.

I know dating you wasn't a mistake, but if we don't make it, I can't see a way forward—that's what's terrifying. I've never been one to let fear hold me back, and I'm not going to start now.

Sixth date recap:

Perfection in every way. Hopefully, I won't let you down for date seven, but even if I do, remember I'll spend the rest of my life trying to make it up to you if you'll let me. See you Thursday, Bex.

He still doesn't see it. Everything became about him because nothing brings me more happiness than when he is happy. It's clear Tristan loves me—I only wish he'd open his eyes and see how much I adore him. The two of us belong together.

Non-date:

Bexley,

Today, I figured out what would be the perfect seventh date. I took a half day off from work, caught up with an old acquaintance, and heard a love story for the ages. If there was ever a sign we're on the right track, that would have been the one.

When Adam picked me up, I was excited to meet up with you. Adam told me Sasha was working, so we decided to go to Just an Illusion for pool and darts. Plus, he'd heard a rumor Eli was going to be there, and I was even more excited. I know how much you love him. It was going to be a great night.

Imagine my surprise when you walked in with Finn. His hand pressed against the small of your back was the first of many betrayals. After I told you about my parents, you could've told me you had feelings for him, Bex. You didn't need to pretend to dislike him, and you really didn't need to put on a show about how you felt about me. Unless you were trying to make him jealous, and if that's the case, well done.

As the evening progressed, I watched the two of you with rapt attention. I tried calling you, and it went straight to voicemail. You seemed content to stay in your bubble with him. Did you need that liquid courage to admit to yourself you had feelings for him? Probably, because there was no shortage of affection between the two of you.

If you haven't already figured it out—date seven is off. Somehow, I don't think that will bother you. It's become quite clear you aren't as into me as I am you.

The saddest part of this whole thing is that tonight I really need my best friend, and she isn't available. We fucked this entire thing up, Bex, and for that, I'm sorry. I'm leaving for a few days, and I'm going to be looking for a new place to live. I can't exist in the same space as you. Not when you're all I see when I close my eyes. My rational mind knew it was over when the two of you walked into the bar together, but my heart hasn't received the memo yet.

Be happy, Bex. It's all I've ever wanted for you.
Tristan

As tears stream down my cheeks, I dial Tristan's number. It rings and rings before going to voicemail. He's avoiding me.

"Tristan." His name falls from my lips on a sob. Maybe he'll realize how messed up I am. "We have a lot to talk about. I just read your date notes, and I . . . please don't leave me, Tris. Don't move out and don't ever say I'm not available for you. I will be there for you until my dying breath. Call me, or better yet, come home . . ."

I keep rereading his last note. I'm so angry with him for not talking to me at the bar. I understand why he didn't, sort of, but it's not an excuse. I have so much more to say to him, so I call him again. I'll fill his voicemail if I have to.

"Tris, please think about this rationally. We were in a public place. A place the two of us and our friends frequent often. Go to Just an Illusion and ask Sasha; I'm pretty sure they hooked up last night."

And another one.

"Tristan, this is ridiculous. In ten years, you've never ignored me. I deserve more from you than this, and so does our friendship. Do you want to know what was happening when I had my head on Finn's shoulder? When he had his arm wrapped around mine? Besides the alcohol hitting me fast, thanks to Sasha, I was singing your praises. All night, I talked his ear off about you. I told him more things than were appropriate for co-workers, but I couldn't help it. You were all that was on my mind. This is the happiest I've ever been, and I know you felt the same."

After the last message, I go into my room, retrieve my dating journal, and come back to Tris's bed. I've got one more entry to make.

Tris,

You made a few non-date entries so now I'm going to make one from the night I showed Finn around, and my life fell apart.

The good parts:

Finn coming clean and explaining why he acted like a territorial ass. He apologized, and I took him at his word. He respected my relationship with you.

Seeing a side of Finn that was fun and watching him and Sasha flirt all night

As the alcohol kicked in, all I could think of was you. Finn and Sasha thought it was hilarious. I was like a love-sick puppy. Every word out of my mouth was "Tristan this," and "Tristan that."

Watching Eli play a set. It doesn't matter how old I get, he'll always ignite the inner teenager within.

Going home with a plan. I desperately wanted date seven to be a slumber party and for it to happen last night. I missed you terribly and wanted to connect with you. I had this crazy idea we could stay up all night talking and make love at dawn to bring in not only the new day, date eight but also the rest of our lives.

The bad parts:

You failed to give me the benefit of the doubt. This might be the worst dating fuck-up of all my dates ever, and it kills me that it came from you. I know what you saw and how terribly that must have hurt, but I also know how I felt and how truly innocent everything you witnessed was. Instead of coming down and talking to me, you treated me how you would treat a stranger. Even if our relationship isn't strong enough yet to deserve more, our friendship should've been. You're not the only one who's devastated.

Coming home and you being gone. I didn't know the gravity of what went down until the following morning, but my poor drunken heart was shattered when I realized you weren't home.

Learning how badly I'd hurt you. I wasn't in the wrong completely, but I'll own my part in it. I'd never hurt you that way intentionally, and I think you know that deep down.

Not calling you. This is one hundred percent on me. I was selfish. I didn't want you or Finn to have each other's numbers. I should have used a bar phone or Sasha's, or even the drunk guy next to me, who practically knocked me off my stool and straight into Finn.

You believing the worst in us. One of the things that makes me happy about dating my best friend is that we are stronger together. There is only one thing about me other people know that you don't. If you want to know what it is, you're going to have to talk to me.

You moving out. This is unacceptable and completely disrespectful. I hope you're speaking from fear and not from your heart. If you don't want to date anymore, that sucks, but we'll get past it. Tossing ten years of friendship down the drain because you got your feelings hurt is shitty. I would never do that to you.

You canceled date seven. I'm going to give you some grace on this one because you were drinking and things escalated. In my mind, date seven is temporarily postponed and will be re-addressed at a later time.

Non-date recap:

It really sucked. But here are a few things that don't:

The way you kiss me. That really, really doesn't suck. You can knock that off your list of worries.

The way you look at me as if I'm the only person you see. It's obvious I've been dating all the wrong men, but that's okay because they led me to you.

You're the only person I know who hates dancing as much as I do. This fact alone makes us best friends for life.

No matter how upset I am at you, I forgive you.

No matter how upset you are at me, you'll forgive me. Maybe you already have.

No matter how crappy this learning experience is, we will grow from it and become better friends. Failure is not an option.

There is no one in the world I want in my life more than you. You're the person I want to share my secrets with, tell my problems to, and live my best life with.

I could go on for days, but I'm crying too hard and opt to curl up in Tristan's bed instead. If he doesn't call me tomorrow, I'm going back to his office. I've got a plan, but today, I just need to be sad.

Seventeen

Tristan

The incessant pounding on my door wakes me up. I don't even bother throwing on clothes as I stumble to see who it is. When I crack it open, Adam's smug grin is staring back at me.

I turn around and head back to my bed, and he follows me inside.

"Nice boxers."

"Fuck you," I mutter, and he tsks at me.

"If you paid me any attention, you'd notice I have coffee and breakfast for you, although by now it's more like linner."

My brain isn't working yet, but I do reach out and take the coffee he's offering. "What the hell is linner?"

"Damn, you're dense. Lunch and dinner combined? Linner. It's three in the afternoon, Tris. Have you really been asleep all day?"

The scent of coffee reminds me of Bexley, since coffee is her favorite food group, but I push the thought away and take a sip. I have a lot to do today, and apparently, I've lost most of it.

I answer him after I swallow. "I didn't sleep much last night, and I got up early to call Rudy and cancel tonight's date."

Adam takes a seat by the window after letting some light into the room. I blink as my eyes adjust, and he shakes his head. "You're being ridiculous, and I mean that in the most loving of ways."

"Thanks," I mutter but reach for the breakfast he brought.

"I've talked to Rita, and Bexley, and Sasha. I took the day off work to do your recon. I know right now you're all up in your feelings, but what I can't figure out is why. Tell me or don't—I don't really care right now. You need to fix this before you lose Bexley for good."

I put the sandwich down and take a deep breath. "I'm moving out."

"Then you deserve to lose her."

"She made that choice!" The smug look he's wearing is really pissing me off.

"No, she didn't. I'm tired of playing the middleman here. I'm going to give this to you straight: you've got your head up your ass on this one, Tris."

"Were you not sitting right next to me last night?"

He leans forward, elbows on his knees. "I was, and for the first time in my life, I fully understand the concept of the way things looking not being what they appear to be. I put in the work this morning, and I had answers in less than two hours. Bexley adores you, Tris, and she's a wreck. I've spent the last ten years watching you piss away every opportunity to have the girl of your dreams, so if you fuck this up, I don't ever want to hear you mention her name again."

"So what? You're team Bexley on this one?"

I'm pissed. *Why is he defending her?*

Adam throws his arms up in the air and yells, "Why not? She didn't do anything wrong except get overserved without her knowledge! Sasha feels awful. And for the record, Sasha fucked Finn last night on her break. Let that sink in."

My mind is working hard to wrap around that detail. That's . . . new.

"Look, you're hungover and working through your shit. I get it. Listen to your messages. Be mad if you want to be. Stay here through the weekend like you planned, but don't do anything else stupid. You already canceled date seven, which was the dumbest thing ever."

"I'm not in any kind of frame of mind to even attempt taking Bex out."

"Well, she's probably not in the frame of mind to go out, but a phone call might help put her at ease."

Speaking of phones, I power mine on, and the notifications ping like crazy. It looks like they're all from her. She even texted me, and Bexley doesn't text if she doesn't have to.

My eyes meet Adam's, and he shrugs. "Told you, she's a mess. Maybe you guys haven't said it yet, but you have to know she's head over heels in love with you, Tris."

I groan as I scroll through the messages. Bex isn't the only one trying to get ahold of me; so is my office. Looks like Bex went there earlier. "Fuck, Adam. What am I doing?"

"I don't know, but you need to figure it out."

"How can I be wrong about last night? I felt each one of their flirty touches in my gut."

He laughs. "Maybe I shouldn't have given you the alcohol. I need to own my part in how fucked up the night went. Once I realized you weren't going to talk to her, I should have gone down and told them we were there. But try to remember exactly what you saw last night; maybe it will help calm you down because one thing I can assure you is that they didn't have any shared caresses. That is such a pussy word, by the way."

I finish off my coffee before responding. "Pussy word or not, you know what it means."

Adam's phone vibrates across the table, and he wears a self-satisfied smirk after checking it. "Are you going home tonight?"

"No. I need time to process and think."

"All right. If you're still processing tomorrow, call me, and I'll tell you what this message says. I gotta go because even though I took the day off for you, I'm not about to miss the opportunity for a booty call. You know how to get ahold of me if you want to talk."

"Thanks, Adam."

"You're my boy, Tris—that isn't going to change. But if you could get your head straight, so everyone doesn't think my best friend is an idiot, that would be great."

"Yeah, I'll get right on that. God forbid you be reflected in a negative light."

Adam pauses at the door. "Seriously, don't fuck this up. It's going to affect us all if you do."

After Adam leaves, I take a shower and brush my teeth. I pull out my laptop to check my email, but I can't concentrate. My phone beckons, and even though I don't want to hear her voice, ten years of friendship can't be ignored. I need to know she's okay.

Each message that plays, she goes through a range of emotions. Calm, frantic, hysterical, sobbing, and worst of all, devastated. I scroll through her texts, and the last one I can't ignore.

Bexley: At least text me back and let me know you're alive.

Me: I'm alive.

It's all I've got for her until I figure this out. The one thing I'm trying to remind myself of is that Bex isn't my mom, and she isn't a cheater. These issues are mine, and while I'm upset with her right now, I'm more upset with myself. I can't shake how last night affected me, but I'm not so stubborn that I can't admit it isn't all her fault. If I could go back and do it all again, I would have walked down there the second they got to the bar.

I spend the next hour looking for apartments, and then I spend another two hours looking for houses. If I'm going to move, it doesn't make sense to rent anymore. I'm not sure what is going to happen with Bex and me, but the more I think about it, distance doesn't seem like a bad idea. We've spent the past four years living together, and maybe, if we truly want to date and make a relationship happen, living apart is a better idea.

I've saved some links and emailed a realtor, and I'm ready to dive into some work when my stomach growls. I look over at the rest of the sandwich Adam brought and eliminate that as an option.

I could call Bex, extend an olive branch, and listen to her side of the story. Instead, I order room service and work through the night. It's better to push Bex off. With my emotions all over the place, the last thing I want to do is talk to her and make things worse.

Friday afternoon comes, and I still haven't spoken to Bex, and she hasn't tried contacting me since yesterday.

After going through some resumes for the CFO position, I head down to the hotel gym to work off some of my aggression. I'm thinking about going to the office to do some game testing. Being in this hotel is making me stir-crazy.

An attractive woman is using the elliptical across from my treadmill. She watches me with a lascivious gaze, and I do my best to keep my eyes on the television and not her bouncing breasts. The last thing I want or need right now is another complication in my life.

"Thought I'd find you here." Adam stands in front of me, and I'm thankful for the distraction.

"You know me well."

"Talk to Bexley yet?"

"Nope."

He shoves his hands in his pockets. "Gonna do something about that?"

"Not planning on it today."

Adam smiles. "So tomorrow morning over pancakes at Rudy's then?"

Fuck . . . I slow my pace to start my cool-down. "It honestly hadn't crossed my mind."

"I figured as much. If you don't go tomorrow, your friendship will never recover. Rudy's on a Saturday morning is an institution for the two of you, even if you don't go every week like you used to. I guarantee you, tomorrow, she'll be there." Adam waits quietly as I wipe down the machine and myself.

"Did she send you here to remind me?" I ask.

We walk side by side back to my room. "Nah, thought you might want to grab a drink in the bar. It's Friday night, and Rita's spending it with Bex, and Ben and Jerry."

"Yeah, that sounds good. Let me shower, and then we can eat and have a couple of drinks."

The second I come out of the bathroom after my shower, Adam flips out on me.

"Are you serious with this shit, Tris?" he asks. He's got my computer on his lap, and I've left the real estate links up.

"I'm allowed to plan my future, Adam."

"Are you including Bex in these plans?"

I pocket my phone and my wallet and sit down to put on my shoes. "Eventually, I'll have to tell her."

Adam closes the computer and sets it aside. "I feel like I don't even know who you are right now."

"That makes two of us."

We go down to the bar in complete silence and choose a booth so we can get food. Once we've ordered, and we have our drinks, I figure it's time to explain my thought process. "I love Bex. I think I always have. She's the only one who knows that when we were in high school, my mom had an affair."

Adam's eyes widen, but he motions for me to continue.

"I guess I never said anything because it was hard enough to deal with myself. I didn't want anyone else judging my dad for staying or my mom for what happened. The guy could have been Finn. Same swagger, arrogance, etcetera."

"Damn, Tris. That's rough."

I pick at the label on my bottle. "It is what it is, but it's why this whole thing has gotten to me. I told Bex everything a few days ago because I figured she should know why I disliked him so much."

"And when she seemed to be into him, it fucked with you even more."

"Exactly."

Adam motions the waitress for two more beers and finishes his off. "If that hadn't happened, would you be considering moving?"

"No, but the more I think about falling in love with Bex, the more I wonder if living together is doing us a disservice."

"How so?"

"She's never had a relationship. Shouldn't she get to experience it the right way? The nerves, the anticipation, all of the firsts? Not to mention, we already live together. We have to be blurring a million different lines."

"You're overthinking this. I'm not saying the idea doesn't have some merit, but Bex has been on more dates than anyone I know. The two of you have built one of the strongest foundations I've ever seen for a relationship. I can't help but feel like you're going to fuck it all up if you do this."

I'm still nervously picking at the label of my bottle. "Everything is already fucked up."

"It doesn't have to be. Look, man, I'm no relationship expert, but I've got some experience with the two of you. Just talk to her. You guys will figure this out one way or another."

The waitress brings our beers and burgers, and we dig in. Once we've finished eating, we shoot the shit for a bit longer until Adam needs to leave.

"All right, man, I'm out," Adam announces.

"Early night for you."

He scoffs. "Nah, just need a nap before my late night booty call."

"Things are getting serious with you and Rita?"

Adam reaches into his pocket and pulls out his phone. "We're taking things slow, but not letting the dating dictate our fucking. She's the female version of me, so it's cool. And this is a reminder for you." He holds his phone out to me, and it's a text from Bexley. She sent it yesterday.

Bexley: Thank you for being a good friend. Can you please remind Tristan we have breakfast Saturday morning at Rudy's? Usual time, usual booth. If he gives you shit, remind him there isn't anything that can't be worked out over chocolate chip pancakes.

"This is why you tracked me down tonight?" I ask with a frustrated sigh.

He pockets his phone. "I tracked you down because that's what friends do—we check in. But I also told you yesterday if you hadn't talked to Bex, I'd tell you what the message was about. Two birds, one stone. I'm doing all the heavy lifting in this crazy little triad of ours and getting none of the fringe benefits. Except dinner and drinks. Those are on you—it's the least you can do."

I laugh for the first time in two days. "Get out of here . . . and thanks, Adam, for trying to pull my head out of my ass."

"Did it work?"

"We'll see."

After paying the bill, I go back to my room and dive into work emails and more resumes. There's one that stands out among them all, and normally, I'd discuss it with Bex, but I can't.

Not being able to talk to her about something as simple as a resume leads me down a rabbit hole of other things I can't talk to her about. Maybe Adam is right, and I need to clear the air between us. My world revolves around Bexley—without her, life doesn't make sense. But whenever I think of her, my chest aches, and I can't catch my breath. If this is what true love feels like, I'm not sure I want it anymore.

I've been sitting outside Rudy's for fifteen minutes. Bexley is inside, and I feel more like an asshole than anything.

When I enter the diner, Rudy himself is at the counter, and he motions for me to follow him. "You kept the pretty lady waiting. It gave me the opportunity to keep her company for a bit. I was disappointed you didn't make it the other night."

I pull an envelope from my pocket and pass it to him. "A deal is a deal. I was disappointed as well, but I think it was for the best."

"I think it was my Mary's way of wanting in on the fun. Today is her birthday, after all. Enjoy your breakfast." He pats my shoulder and walks away, leaving me standing awkwardly at our table.

It hasn't even been two full days since I've seen her, and my first instinct is to lean down and hug her. Breathing becomes easier in her proximity, but she's always had that effect on me. She doesn't look like she's been sleeping well, but she's still absolutely gorgeous. I wasn't sure I could do this, but even though it hurts, I know this is where I need to be. The thought of losing her stabs me in the heart as our eyes meet for the first time in days.

Bex motions for me to sit as she stirs her coffee. The waitress who delivered my note to Bex the other day brings me a cup of coffee.

The waitress pulls out her order pad. "Ready for those chocolate chip pancakes now?"

"Yes, please," Bex answers, and I also give the waitress an agreeing nod. When she leaves the table, Bex looks up at me. "You look tired," she says wearily.

"So do you."

"Always so quick to point out my flaws," she counters with a slight grin.

"Just calling 'em like I see 'em."

"Tristan, I should explain." She pauses and takes a deep breath.

"No, don't. I rushed to judgment when I had no right. We're not exclusive, and you didn't do anything wrong. I'm just . . . overprotective when it comes to you."

Our pancakes arrive quickly, delivered by Rudy himself. "For my favorite lovebirds on one of my favorite days. The two of you give me hope for the future. Your breakfast is on the house this morning." He tilts his head up to the ceiling after putting our plates down. "Happy Birthday, Mary. Thanks for the sign."

Bex opens her mouth to argue, and I give her a slight shake of the head. "Thank you, Rudy, and Happy Birthday, Mary."

"Happy Birthday, Mary," Bex adds, and Rudy remains smiling as he walks away.

We eat mostly in silence, and it's the most uncomfortable situation I've ever been in with her.

"Bex, why did you submit your resume for the CFO job yesterday?" I ask.

"Going there already?" She reaches down for her purse and then stands.

"You're just walking out on me?"

She leans down and kisses the top of my head. Her apricot fragrance wraps around me. "You know what they say about leaving them wanting more? Show up for our date, and I'll answer you."

"What date?"

"You'll see. Finish your coffee, Tris. It will all become clear."

Once Bex exits the diner, our waitress brings me a notebook. "The two of you are so sweet, always leaving each other love notes."

When I open it, there is a letter tucked into the book with a note that says, "read me first."

Dear Tristan,

The past few days have been an awakening. Not necessarily a pleasant one, at times, but I think a much-needed one all the same.

The first thing I want to address is your broken promise. We agreed to seven dates. In fact, if I remember correctly, you're the one who insisted on all seven being completed.

Due to the circumstances, I'm giving you a pass. This breakfast was officially date seven. Maybe it wasn't the best date on record, but we were both here, we had a meal, and exchanged a few words (I'm only leaving these papers if this actually happened). Consider your obligation fulfilled.

In your dating notes, you mentioned wanting to know why our dates went from being focused on me to being focused on you. It's no secret I've been on a lot of dates. When you proposed dating me and allowing me to choose what I wanted to do, I felt special. Your attention to detail is astounding, and you seemed genuinely happy when I was happy. I wanted to know what that felt like.

Addictive, that's what. All the ridiculous and sappy things my mom told me over the years finally made sense. How she would say making my dad a plate or a drink would bring her joy. Or letting him watch his favorite show while she sat next to him and read a book. I could understand it in such a broader context because making you happy brings me joy, Tristan. You've been making women happy in your relationships for years. It's probably

171

why you're so good at the details, but this was my first try and hopefully not my last.

Ten years ago, we became best friends, and I hope that never changes. Now we need to discuss the elephant in the room—Finn. Believe it or not, I think under different circumstances you and he could have been friends. In our lifetime, there are going to be more Finns and more Marias. They'll look different and have different names, but undoubtedly, there will be people in our lives who will find us attractive. They'll flirt and encroach on our space because not everyone respects boundaries.

The good part about it is that we don't have to let them upset our balance. Our bond is stronger than a fleeting attraction. Even while drunk, you were the only one I talked about. We're solid—at least I hope we are. You have to let go of the past. Your parents' history can't define our future. You can't let it dictate if you believe in someone or not. And I have to abide by the same rules. I can't keep comparing everything to the rare and incredible bond my parents have. It isn't fair to me, and it's not fair to anyone I may have a future with. Dating roulette is officially over.

I'm going to try and date like a normal person from here on out. No expectations, no automatic strikes against anyone, and no more trial period with rules on intimacy or anything else. It's time I grow up and become deserving of my soul mate.

However, since you are the last contestant of dating roulette, it's imperative I ask you a question. You're the person who has made it the farthest, and I'd be honored if you'd like to go on another date with me tonight. We can call it date eight or a new beginning, as long as you answer the following question correctly.

My best friend, Tristan Xavier Jacobs, is the most important person in my life. If you're going to date me, you have to accept him. Is that something you can do?

If the answer to this question is yes, please come to our/my apartment this evening at seven p.m. sharp. I'll be wearing your favorite dress, and you should wear whatever makes you happy. Fair warning: the theme this evening is romance. If this isn't the direction you want our relationship to go in, please text me to decline the invitation. But if you want this as much as I do, please come home. I miss you, Tris.

    All my love,
    Bexley

Once I finish her letter, I flip through page after page of her dating notes. These are not at all what I expected, but they're everything I could've hoped for. I'm not sure why it surprises me. Bexley is nothing short of amazing. I was a fool for leaving and for worrying about Finn. Her love for me shines through on each page. It's time to make this right once and for all.

Eighteen

Bexley

After smoothing down the skirt of Tristan's favorite dress, I slip on my heels. He hasn't texted me, but I'm still worried he may not come tonight. I waited in the parking lot for about fifteen minutes before pulling away. He never came out, and I hope that means he was busy reading my words to him.

Our breakfast was awkward and uncomfortable. It wasn't the seventh date I'd had in mind for us, but in a way, I think it was fitting. My dating habits were out of control, and Tristan should've never been a part of the vicious cycle. I was so concerned about finding perfection that I never realized it was staring me in the face the entire time. Tristan should've been the exception to the rule, and in a way, he was, but I hope after tonight, he will be for sure.

The two of us royally screwed things up, but losing Tristan even for a short period made me realize how lucky I am to have him in my world. If things had gone differently at Rudy's, I had another version of the letter to give him. One that put emphasis on our friendship and let him off the hook for any romantic future. I went there prepared for either outcome, but my emotions got the best of me when I went to my car—I cried tears of joy that we might still have a chance.

The timer on the oven dings, and I hurry into the kitchen to take the lasagna out. It's one of the few things I make well from scratch, and it's also Tristan's favorite. I've already made a salad, and I have some garlic rolls in the warmer. It's nearly seven, and I check my phone for the millionth time. Still no text. I hope that means he's coming. He wouldn't wait till the last possible second, would he?

I'm a nervous wreck, pacing around the kitchen. At five after, I'm about to pop open a bottle of wine. Maybe he isn't coming after all.

I'm so consumed by my thoughts I jump when the doorbell rings. It better not be Adam.

I look out the peephole to find Tristan, and when I open the door, he flashes me a heartwarming smile.

I motion for him to come inside. "Why are you ringing the doorbell? This is your apartment too . . . isn't it?"

He's carrying a vase full of tulips and has a bottle of wine precariously tucked under his arm. He leans in and kisses me on the cheek. He looks edible in his slacks, button-up shirt, and tie.

"These are for you." Tris passes me the flowers and pulls the wine free for a more secure hold.

"Thank you." I look at him expectantly, waiting for his answer.

"It's our apartment, but I would like to talk about that later. I rang the bell so we could start this date off on the right foot. A proper greeting at the beginning of a date sets a good first impression."

Butterflies take flight deep in my stomach. "Is that the direction we're going in? First-date territory?"

"Are you always so excitable on a date?" He flashes me a grin that shows off his sexy dimple. All right, he can tease me . . . for now.

After making room for the flowers on our entry table, we make our way into the kitchen. He goes to work opening the wine while I plate our dinners.

He sniffs the air and inhales deeply. "This looks and smells incredible, Bex. You must have cooked all day."

"It's fine; I wanted to. Now can you answer my question?" My answers are abrupt, but he takes them in stride.

He pulls out my chair as if we're in a restaurant and kisses the top of my head. "You're always so impatient."

"Can you blame me? The past few days have been rough."

"For me too. You were right; we focused too much on the dates and not enough on what matters. I want to change that."

The wine he brought is incredible, and when I hum my appreciation, his eyes light up. Damn, I've missed him. "How do we change it?"

"For starters, we communicate. How about we eat and then move this conversation into the living room?"

"Okay." It's a guarantee he's not going to eat and run. He devours his food quickly, and I'm eager to serve him seconds. "Have you been eating?"

"Hotel food for the most part. It's been decent but nothing like this. Thank you for cooking."

Between the wine and the smoldering gaze he's giving me, I'm a bit flushed. "You're welcome." I push my plate away, completely stuffed, and I nurse my wine while he finishes. "Thank you for reading my notes and for coming tonight. I wasn't sure . . . well, it doesn't matter because you're here."

He wipes his mouth and carries our plates to the sink. Tristan grabs the bottle of wine and his glass, and I follow his lead. Once we're settled on the couch together, my butterflies are back. They're a combination of nerves and excitement.

"When I left, I was in a dark place. Leaving was good for me because it gave me time to think. One of the things I'm worried about is living together and dating." He follows his confession with a gulp of wine.

I'm shocked. "Why?"

Tristan reaches for my hand and squeezes it. "It seems to me the dating experience is important to you. I want you to have space and also be able to get excited about seeing your boyfriend. Have the ability to prepare for dates without me in your space."

He is so overthinking this. "We lived apart in college, Tris. I've been there and done that. Not long-term with someone but enough to know what I'd be missing or not. We've lived together for almost five years now, and I'm happy."

"Are you sure?"

"Were you happy the past few days?" I ask. He hesitates and then shakes his head. "Me either. I was more miserable than I've ever been. I'm not above begging you to stay. I didn't realize it was possible to miss someone as much as I missed you. The lack of communication killed me. We've been apart before, but we've never lost communication." I put my wine on the table, and he tucks me into his side.

"I'm sorry, Bex."

"Me too. I want this with you. I know what my life feels like with you and without you. With you, is so much better."

He traces my lips with his fingers and looks down at me. "Angel, why did you send your resume to my office?"

"Kiss me, and I'll tell you."

He lowers his mouth to mine, and I wrap my arm around his neck. I part my lips and sigh into his mouth as our kiss intensifies. We take our time, exploring each other with careful precision.

Tristan pulls back, and I exhale softly. I need him now more than ever.

"Why, Bex?" he asks.

"On Thursday, I was freaking out. The first place I went was to your office. I walked through and saw everyone hard at work on the games. Something clicked; I saw everything in a new light. Your employees are happy, Tris, and your office flows in a way most people are never fortunate enough to experience in their workplace. Then I got upstairs to the murals."

"You and those murals." A grin kicks up at the corner of his mouth.

"They're my favorite because each one of them comes from here." I place my hand over his heart and feel the rapid thudding of his heartbeat. "You create worlds in your mind where people lose themselves. In a way, your office is like that too. You want the best for everyone, and you take care of your people."

I reach for my wine, needing a sip before continuing. "I like my job, and I love the building and its perks."

"I'm just another numbers geek there. My boss only knows my name because I've worked my ass off to get where I am. I'm one of the few who goes above and beyond, which is why he asked me to show Finn around—I'm dependable." I pause to gauge his reaction to my mentioning Finn so soon. Fortunately, he doesn't seem bothered. "With your company, I'd feel a part of something greater. But also, it would give me greater purpose because I would be building something for someone I love. While you were gone, I felt lost. I don't know if this is going to work between us or not, but if I'm losing you, if you're moving out, I need to be able to recoup my time with you. What better way than to help you continue building something great?"

He takes my glass away and puts it next to his. "Did you just admit you love me?"

My cheeks heat. "Yes. I know you saw it in my notes this morning but are too gentlemanly to bring it up. It's all I've wanted to tell you since you left, but you deserve so much more than for me to say it during an argument."

"Disagreement," he corrects.

I kick off my shoes and hike up my skirt so I can straddle him. Once I'm settled in his lap, I cup his cheeks in my hands and lay my heart on the line. "I love you, Tristan. I've loved you for ten years, but over the past few months, my heart opened wider for you. I'm not sure I understood it, but it's why I seized the opportunity to flirt with you the night of your pizza delivery incident."

"I think I understand." He runs his hands through my hair, and I sigh contentedly.

"Do you? I'm in this pretty deep, Mr. Jacobs. Especially after the uncertainty of the past few days. I may easily become a stage-five clinger."

Tris pulls me close and pecks me on the lips. "Will you still go to scary amusement parks with me?"

"If you'll protect me and buy me a funnel cake."

"Would you leave me if I wore tasseled loafers?" His eyes sparkle mischievously.

"Never, but I might make fun of you and take you shopping to point out a more appropriate footwear choice."

"Will you still work for me if I admit I love you, too?"

My breath catches as my heart skips a beat. "Until the end of time."

"Do you think we're moving too fast?"

Our eyes lock, and I shake my head. "I think this has been the slowest coupling in history. Everyone else saw what we were too afraid to admit to ourselves."

"Did you wear my favorite dress because you love me?"

As I slip my fingers through his curls, I shake my head again as I lower my lips to his ear. "I wore your favorite dress because I want you to peel it off me before you fuck me."

He groans, and I feel his hardness beneath me. "Your room or mine?" His hands wrap around my ass as he stands, and I wrap my legs around his waist.

"Yours. We need to make new memories in there because that's where I slept while you were gone. You are back, Tris, right?"

He stops next to his bed, and I slide down every hard plane of his body before my feet hit the ground. "I'm never leaving you again. In fact, I might just put your desk in my office, and we can share."

"We'd never get any work done. Wait . . . does that mean I have the job?"

Tris runs his thumb over my tiny developing wrinkle. "Was there ever a question? Even if I was angry, I'm not stupid. You're the best thing for my company, Bex, and for me."

"Does your insurance cover plastic surgery? You're giving me a complex about this wrinkle."

He throws back his head and laughs. "Fuck, you're adorable, and for the record, so is this wrinkle." His lips brush over my problem area, and my heart melts. "This tiny little spot on your head is one of my favorite parts of you."

"Why?"

"It's your thinking crease. When you're considering something important or trying to work out something in your head, it appears. Almost like your brain is working so hard it needs a little more space. It gives me insight into what is important to you. Don't ever change it."

"Hmm, we'll see."

"You're perfect just as you are. I can't wait to one day see the crow's feet that will appear here." His fingers trace along the sides of my eye. "Or the laugh lines that will embed themselves here." He moves them down along the side of my nose and mouth. "Other men might see them as imperfections but not me. I'm going to see them as a life well lived."

"Jesus, you're romantic."

He nips my lip with his teeth. "I'm also dirty, but I promise I'll figure out how to find a balance."

"Hmm, this will be interesting."

Tristan turns me in his arms and bites the back of my neck. "If you need me to stop, just say so."

"Are you crazy? Why would I want you to stop? We're finally getting to the good stuff."

Chuckling against my skin, he ever so slowly unzips my dress. He slides the dress down my arms, his mouth never leaving my heated skin.

There isn't a curve from my shoulders to my ass his hands don't explore as he tugs my dress down. Once it's finally free of the swell of my ass, it falls to the floor, and he sighs appreciatively. He kneels and lifts my feet, tossing the dress to the side.

His lips and tongue follow his hands in their exploration of my body. My knees are like jelly, and the needy cries falling from my lips should be embarrassing, but if anyone understands how I feel, it's Tris. He's waited just as long as I have for this.

"Damn, Bex, you have no idea the depraved things I want to do to this ass." He squeezes each cheek hard, and I have to squeeze my thighs together. "Oh no, angel. Don't you fucking hold anything back."

Tristan smacks my ass hard enough that I yelp, but fuck, if I'm not wishing he'd do it again. He slides his hand down the back of my panties and wraps another around my waist, pulling us flush together.

"Are you wet for me?" he asks.

"Yes." My breathless reply comes as his teeth nip my earlobe, and he slips a finger through my wetness.

Tristan groans, slides his hand out of my panties, and turns me in his arms. His gaze rakes over me from head to toe. I've got on a navy demi bra and panties, which match my dress.

His cock tents his pants, and I lick my lips, admiring his body. "You're wearing entirely too many clothes."

"We should fix that," he replies with a smoldering gaze.

I step forward and loosen his tie before reaching for his wrist and unbuttoning his cuff. As I repeat the motion on his other hand, he pulls his tie off and tosses it across the room. When his wrists are free, he begins unbuttoning his shirt.

"I was going to do that for you," I say with a pout.

"I'm quicker," he answers while rapidly working through his buttons.

"Okay then." I drop to my knees and look up at him as I unhook his belt. "Guess I'll start here."

He groans when I press a kiss to his cock through his clothing. His shoes are still on, and once I've got his pants unzipped, they fall around his ankles.

My breath hitches, and I squeeze his muscular thighs while taking in the sight of him in his boxer briefs. He throws his shirt on the floor, and I pull down his briefs and get my first up-close-and-personal look at his hardened dick. Without a second thought, I lick the wetness from the tip. His hands grip my hair, and he arches his hips closer.

"Tristan, I want to taste you."

"It might be fast. This is already better than I'd ever imagined." His confession encourages me to keep going.

I circle the tip of him with my tongue, familiarizing myself with his taste and his ridges. Following the vein down his shaft, I lick and suck as he pulls my hair harder the more I tease him. When I wrap my hand around his shaft, he calls out my name, but it isn't good enough. I want to hear him when he comes down my throat. I work his length with my hand as I lower my mouth around his cock.

"Angel, your mouth is a motherfucking nirvana." His words fuel me to take him deeper, suck him harder, and work him faster. The taste of him is ever-present on my tongue, and I can't get enough. "Bex . . . I'm going to come . . . if you don't want . . ."

Damn it, I do want. I work harder to take more of him, and when he pulses his release, I moan as I take it all.

"Holy shit, Bexley!" he gasps, fighting hard to catch his breath. Once he's fully spent, I slowly remove him from my mouth and look him in the eye before licking every last drop from my lips.

Tristan slips his arms under mine and lifts me to my feet. "Guess I'm not the only dirty one," he quips before slamming his mouth over mine. Our tongues move in relentless tandem, and his hand slips between my legs. He presses against my clit, and I push against him with need.

With one hand, he reaches behind me and unsnaps my bra. When it's undone, he pulls away from our kiss and removes it. Leaning down, he flicks and teases each of my nipples, and I push his head closer as I cry out.

"Get on the bed," he says in his commanding voice, and it has my heart racing. I'll do anything he wants if he says it in that tone.

I lie down as he works to get his shoes and pants off, and I suppress my grin. He's bent over, and the flex of his ass is something else. Unlike my ass, there's no junk in his trunk.

Tristan reaches into the bedside drawer and grabs a strip of condoms.

"Hey." I reach for his wrist, and he kneels next to me on the bed. "I thought we agreed we didn't need them? Or have you been with someone after all?"

My mind races as his finger lands on that spot between my eyebrows. "Stop worrying. I haven't been with anyone. I just didn't want to assume this was something you still wanted."

"We're clean, I'm on birth control, and more than anything, I don't want any barriers. Not with you, Tris."

"Okay." He tosses the condoms onto the nightstand and moves down my body. He slips his fingers into the sides of my panties and pulls them off me. We're both completely naked.

"Wow."

His eyes lock on mine. "Is this okay? Are you weirded out?"

"I wondered if I would be," I admit hesitantly, "but honestly, I've never felt more comfortable with anyone."

"Me either," he confesses before opening my legs. His eyes are still locked on mine, but when his head drops and his tongue slips through my most intimate area, I close my eyes and fall into his bliss.

Each stroke of his tongue brings me higher and higher. He moans against my skin, and as his tongue slips inside me, I buck against him. One of his fingers rubs circles around my clit as he fucks me with his tongue.

"Tristan! Oh God, right there . . . deeper," I cry. He growls louder as I thrust harder against him. I lace my fingers through his hair and push his head where I need him most. My orgasm builds, and my body tingles all over. Sharing this moment with him is a whole new realm of sexual awakening. He slides a finger inside me with his tongue, and my body detonates.

Like a starving man, Tristan sucks and licks my release as I whimper and writhe beneath him. He looks up, and his eyes burn with desire. "You have no idea how long I've wanted to feel you explode on my tongue. Even when we weren't together, there were times when I'd allow myself to imagine it, but the reality is so much better."

"So we're together? You never really clarified what you wanted this to be when I asked you earlier."

He crawls up my body, kissing and caressing his way up until his lips meet mine. "I'm in love with you, Bexley. Mind, body, and soul. We can call this whatever you'd like. Exclusive, boyfriend/girlfriend, engaged—I don't care. As long as we're committed to each other in every way, I'm happy."

"Engaged, huh? Think you need a ring for that. Maybe you should kneel at my feet too." I caress his cheek. "I'm good with us being in a committed relationship."

"Perfect." Tristan positions himself between my legs, and we share a long, languid kiss. His cock presses against my entrance, and I wrap my legs around his waist.

"Make love to me, Tris."

He reaches between us and guides himself to my entrance. As he inches inside me, I gasp and adjust to him.

It's been a while since I've had sex, and Tris is quite bigger than most of the guys I've been with.

"You okay?" Concern fills his features.

"I'm perfect. Kiss me."

As we kiss, my body loosens, and soon Tristan fills me. Our bodies move together like they were made for each other. Tristan and I have become one, and if I have my way, we'll be one for the rest of our lives.

Our slow lovemaking turns frantic as he thrusts into me. Tris bites at my nipples and sucks at the spot he loves on my lower neck, surely leaving another mark. I don't mind; I'm his, and he can use me however he'd like as long as he keeps fucking me this way.

"Put your arms above your head." There he is, the commanding man who lives inside Tris. I was wondering if he was going to come back. I quickly comply, and he nips my lip with his teeth. He growls, "Is someone needy?"

He shifts his body and hitches my leg around his hip. When he thrusts, he hits the spot deep inside I've only ever reached with my vibrator.

"Oh God," I whimper, and his arm tightens around my thigh.

"You didn't answer me." He leans forward, and with his free hand, he grips my wrists. I might bruise. I hope I bruise. I want his marks on my skin so I'll be continuously reminded of his dominance. "Are. You. Needy. Angel?"

He pistons forward, and stars explode behind my eyes. "Yes, yes, oh God, yes!" Wave after wave of pleasure rolls through me as a tsunami of emotions continues to build. He moves deeper and deeper in some kind of rhythmic pattern the gods of erotica must have blessed him with. I'm so close, and as he thrusts again, he squeezes my wrists and bites my nipple. My body explodes, and between my undecipherable cries, he comes as he calls out my name. The pulse of him releasing inside me sets off a flurry of emotions. Without even realizing it, tears are streaming down my cheeks.

Tristan collapses on top of me. Our hearts beat erratically against one another. Being skin to skin with someone has never felt this good.

"Bex, you're crying. Are you okay? Did I hurt you?" He begins to move, but I wrap my arms around him.

"Don't go. I'm perfect. Just . . . overwhelmed?"

His lips briefly meet mine. "I pushed you too fast."

"No, Tristan, I think it's . . ." I'm embarrassed to even say it, but I know with him, I can say anything. "I've never loved anyone I've done this with before." My arm flies over my eyes because even though I shouldn't be embarrassed, I am.

"Bex . . ." He hesitates. Of course he's felt this before.

"Don't, Tris. It's okay. I know I'm not your first love."

When he peels my arm from my face, he's smiling down at me. "But you are. You're the first girl I've ever loved. I've loved you from the moment we met. You set the standard for everything I wanted in a partner. There are different kinds of love, Bexley, but the kind I feel for you— I've never felt this before, and I never want to feel it with anyone else. You're stuck with me, Bexley Marie Scott, and if I'm really lucky, it will be for the rest of my life."

"Wouldn't that make me the lucky one?"

"Maybe it makes us both lucky. After all, we're the final participants of dating roulette."

Epilogue

Tristan

Six months later

Adam's groans carry through the house. Everything echoes in here since it's mostly just boxes right now.

"You guys are grown-ups, and you're not poor. Why didn't you hire movers?" he asks.

He's holding his lower back like a pregnant woman, and Bexley laughs. "Because all we have is boxes, and since we have you, we don't need movers. I can pay you in beer, but I'd have to pay them with cash."

"You're also going to be paying for my massage. Preferably at that place down in the valley, you know the one with the women who . . ."

Rita narrows her eyes at him. "The one with the women who end relationships with a single stroke? Yeah, he knows the one. Let me know if you send him there, Tris, because my office is right across from Finn's now, and I'm sure he wouldn't mind stroking me to my happily-ever-after either."

Adam circles around and scoops Rita into his arms. "You wouldn't dare."

"Try me, hot stuff. Boyfriends of mine don't get massages that finish in happy endings unless I'm the one giving them."

The two of them kiss, and as per their usual, they take it a bit too far in front of Bex and me.

I wave my arms in surrender. "Enough. Go home. Bex and I can take it from here. You guys don't get to christen our house before we do."

Rita giggles and grabs her purse and keys. "You don't have to tell me twice. Happy housewarming, you two!"

They run out the door like two kids ditching school.

"Do you think he loves her?" she asks softly.

I close the door and lock it. "Yes, but not as much as I love you. Happy new home day, angel."

She wraps her arms around me and sighs. "I love you, too."

I lead her over to the giant bean bag we bought to sit on until our furniture is all delivered over the next week. We collapse on it and snuggle together.

We launched a new game at work last week, and it was all hands on deck for a few weeks leading up to it. Having Bexley join us in the office has turned out better than I could've imagined. Role-playing controlling boss and subservient employee after hours has been incredibly fun as well. The company feels complete now. Bex helped me get it up and running, and now it finally feels like a family operation.

Because of all the long hours, we were right up against the clock for our move. Neither of us wanted to pay another month on the apartment when we'd already closed escrow and had our dream home waiting empty for us.

I kiss the top of her head, "Are you as tired as I am?"

She looks up at me with half-closed eyes. "Exhausted. Remind me never to wait until the last minute to pack a place we've lived in for five years. Where did we get all that stuff?"

Yawning, I pull her in even closer. "I'm not sure where it came from, but I'm sure we'll probably accumulate even more now that we're building our future here."

"Nap and then unpack?" she mumbles, already losing the fight to stay awake.

"Sounds like a plan."

"Tristan, I'm starving." Bex kisses my lips before whispering in my ear, "Are you awake?"

"I've got something you can eat." I reach for her hand and lower it to my cock.

She laughs and pushes me away. "You're so wrong, but I still love you."

"You're the one who used her sexual prowess to try to get food."

Bexley sighs. "I think we have eggs, but I don't want to unpack boxes for eggs."

"No unpacking. Go take a shower and put on my favorite dress. It's hanging in the closet. I'm taking you out for dinner. All your toiletries are in our master bathroom already."

"Have I mentioned how much I love you lately?"

"You have, but if you want to show me, we can revisit the blow job discussion later."

"Feed me something amazing, and you've got yourself a deal."

While Bexley gets ready, I head into one of the spare bedrooms where I stored my things earlier and take a shower. I take my time, knowing it doesn't matter how slow I am; she'll still be putting on her makeup when I'm dressed.

I'm wearing the suit I bought when I was in the hotel. I want us to be wearing the same clothes tonight that we wore the first night we made love. Maybe it's superstition, but that was a good night, and I want tonight to be as well.

"You almost ready?" I call out, not used to the echo of the new house.

"Five minutes, babe!"

In the kitchen, I start opening boxes. When I find the pans, I take them out and set them on the counter. I find the plates and do the same. We haven't discussed what goes where, but at least now when she's hungry in the morning, she can make eggs.

Her arms wrap around me from behind. "Thank you for finding those."

"Thank you for making me eggs in the morning when you make yours."

She laughs and releases me.

When I turn around, my breath catches. "You look incredible."

"It's not like you haven't seen me in this dress a hundred times."

"The dress is nice, angel, but you're what makes it special." I finger the diamond necklace she's wearing. It was part of my Christmas gift to her, along with the proposal that we buy a house together.

"Well, you look pretty sexy yourself. Where are we going?"

"It's a surprise, but let's get going."

When we pull up in front of Rudy's, she squeals. "It's like you know me or something. It's dark, though. Are they open?"

We get out of the car, and I take her hand in mine. "They're open for us."

"Tristan . . ."

"Come on, Rudy is waiting."

Sure enough, by the time we get to the door, Rudy has it open and is motioning for us to come inside. "If it isn't my two favorite customers. Welcome to Rudy's After Dark."

Bex giggles as Rudy leads us to the table.

"Your favorite table and your favorite waitress will be right out to take your order." Rudy disappears into the kitchen, and Sandy steps out.

"Coffee?" she asks.

"Yes please, and water too," Bexley replies sweetly.

"You got it," Sandy says with a wink.

Bex reaches across the table and takes my hand in hers. She's smiling from ear to ear.

Sandy brings the drinks and creamer. As soon as they hit the table, Bex opens the sugar. Some things will never change.

"Do I even need to ask what you want to order? Or are we having chocolate chip pancakes all around?" Sandy already knows this answer, but to her credit, she plays along.

"With extra whipped cream," Bexley adds.

"Same," I reply with a shrug, and Sandy shakes her head.

"I used to be able to eat like the two of you. Those were the days."

Once she disappears into the kitchen, Bex arches a brow. "Spill it, Tris. Why are you repeating the date that never happened?"

"This is the date I wanted for you more than anything. Well, for us. It was supposed to be our new beginning. A celebration for us making it through to the end. I thought today was as good a chance as any to recreate what we missed. We're starting our new lives today. New home, and hopefully, the beginning of our forever."

"Tris, our forever started the day we met . . ."

I slide out of the booth and get down on one knee in front of her. Bexley's eyes fly open wider than I've ever seen them, and she gasps before covering her mouth.

I pull the ring box from my pocket and open it. I've had this ring since I bought the suit. Call it wishful thinking, but I knew the only way I was going back home to her that night was if I was all in. I wanted to propose back then, but waiting was the right thing to do. We needed to experience falling in love together instead of documenting our separate journeys to each other in notebooks.

"Bexley Marie Scott, you forced your friendship on me during our sophomore year of high school, and it has by far been the best thing to ever happen to me. You've been my best friend for ten years, but you're also the absolute love of my life. If I promise to spend the rest of my days loving you the way you deserve to be loved, being romantic, commanding, and at times, a bit dirty, as well as supplying you with as many chocolate chip pancakes as you can eat, will you do me the honor of becoming my wife?"

I'm trying to be subtle and not hyperventilate, but this kind of pressure is no joke.

She's nodding, but her mouth is still covered, and tears are streaming down her cheeks. I scoot closer to her and reach for her hand. "I'm going to need you to use your words, angel."

"Yes! Tristan Xavier Jacobs, it took you long enough!"

Now, I understand why she was covering her mouth—I didn't realize she was holding back a scream.

"I've been waiting for you to ask me this since, well . . . I don't know, it seems like ten freaking years, but I'm sure it's only been about six months, give or take."

She launches herself out of the booth and knocks me off balance. We both fall to the floor as I wrap my arms around her.

Rudy peeks his head over the counter and looks down at us. "We might be closed for the night, but remember this is still a family-friendly restaurant. My Mary would have loved this. Congratulations, you two. Pancakes will be out in a jiff."

I pull myself up and then help Bexley. When I take the ring from the box, she does a little happy dance. "You're that excited about the ring?" I ask.

"Put it on me, Tris."

After I slide the ring on her finger, she pulls me into a hug without even looking at it. "The ring is beautiful, but the symbolism is what matters to me. Call me old-fashioned, but knowing you love me enough to make me your wife is what excites me most. I'm probably setting back feminism a hundred years, but I feel like the only thing I've ever needed in my life was to be loved by you."

"I know exactly how you feel," I reply. Our mouths brush together, but Rudy clears his throat and interrupts us as he delivers our dinner.

"If the two of you want the diner for your wedding shower or reception, you let me know. It's nice to see some new love christen the place."

Bexley tears up. "Thanks, Rudy, we'd be honored. Let us get back to you once we figure things out."

I'm pretty sure I see the old man blink back tears of his own before heading into the kitchen.

"Would you want that?" I ask.

"Maybe? At least the shower? We're not high-maintenance people, Tris, and this place has so many memories for us. Especially now. And who knows? Someday, maybe we'll bring our kids here for breakfast too."

While the two of us share our excitement and talk about when we want to get married, I can't help but think about what she said. One day she wants to bring our kids here. I've always wanted kids but only thought about it in the abstract.

She leans in close. "Tris, are you okay? Where did your mind go?" Her little thinking wrinkle is starting to appear.

"My mind went to babies with you."

"Oh." She's blushing. "Is that a bad thing?"

"Nope. In fact, I think we should go home and get a jumpstart on practicing. I can't think of anything better than a few more Bexleys in the world."

She reaches for my hand. "I can. If the world has more Bexleys, we have to give it more Tristans to even the balance."

"Who are we? In the past six months, we've fallen in love, bought a house, and gotten engaged."

Bexley pushes our plates out of the way and leans across the table to kiss me. "We're the people we were always meant to be. The universe brought us together so we could become the best versions of ourselves. I can't wait to see how our story ends."

"It's going to be incredible, and I'm going to savor every moment of *us* from beginning to end."

She sighs before running her finger through some whipped cream on her plate and sucking it into her mouth. "You're so romantic, Tris."

She probably wouldn't say that if she could see my cock. I lean forward, and we lock eyes. "Keep sucking the cream from your finger like that, and romantic is the last thing I'm going to be."

Bexley's eyes dilate. "Don't ever stop using that voice. It does the best things to me."

"Never." In the past few months, I've learned exactly what it does to her, and I can't wait to get home. I step out of the booth and hold out my hand. "Are you ready to start making memories?"

She slips her hand in mine. "I've treasured every moment we've spent together since we met." Bexley leans close to my ear, and whispers, "Use that voice on me when we get home, though, and I'll give you something you'll never forget."

"You're already the most unforgettable part of my life."

"And you're mine. Thank you for being my best friend, Tris."

As we exit the diner, I pull her into my arms. "The best decision I ever made. I love you, Bexley. Thank you for choosing to spend your life with me."

"You're smart, handsome, romantic, and seriously gifted between the sheets. I'd be a fool to let you go."

"Is that all?"

She smiles up at me. "I'd also be lost without you."

"There's my romantic girl—I knew she'd show up eventually."

"Only for you, Tris."

"Well, as the reigning champion of dating roulette, I think that's a fitting prize."

Bexley groans. "You're never going to let me live this down, are you?"

"Are you kidding? This will make *the* best story for our grandkids."

"I like the sound of that."

"Me too, angel. Me too."

Thank you for reading *Dating Roulette*. I hope you enjoyed Tristan and Bexley's story. If you'd like to read more about Just an Illusion, Eli Watts, and Sasha, you can find them in The Illusion Series.

To keep up with release information, updates, pre-orders, and more, please consider joining my mailing list.

http://www.dkellyauthor.com/mailing-list/

If you'd like to join my reader group, we'd love to have you! Please visit Dee's Dirty Divas on Facebook -

https://www.facebook.com/groups/239952459522719/

To purchase Just an Illusion – Side A or other books by D. Kelly please visit –

http://www.dkellyauthor.com/all-books

Dear Readers

The most important thing you can do for the authors you love is to leave a review and tell your friends how much you enjoyed their book. If you wouldn't mind taking a few moments to rate and review this book, I would greatly appreciate it.

Sincerely,

Dee Kelly

About
D. Kelly

D. Kelly

D. Kelly, author of The Acceptance Series, The Illusion Series, and standalone companion novels *Chasing Cassidy* and *Sharing Rylee*, was born and raised in Southern California. She's a wife, mom, dog lover, taxi, problem fixer, and extreme multi-tasker. She married her high school sweetheart and is her kids' biggest fan.

Kelly has been writing since she was young and took joy in spinning stories to her childhood friends. Margaritas and sarcasm make her smile, she loves the beach but hates the san, and she believes Starbucks makes any day better.

A contemporary romance writer, D. Kelly's stories revolve around friendship and the bond it creates, strengthening the love of the people who share it. For all things D. Kelly, you can visit her website: http://www.dkellyauthor.com

The Acceptance Series –
Breaking Kate – Book One
Catching Kate – Book 1.5
Releasing Kate- Book Two
Loving Kate – Book Three
Christmas with the Houstons – Book Four

Standalone Novels
Chasing Cassidy
Sharing Rylee
The Evolution of Us
The Last Resort Motel – Room 13
Dating Roulette

The Illusion Series
Just an Illusion – Side A
Just an Illusion – The B Side
Just an Illusion – EP
Just an Illusion – Unplugged
Just an Illusion – Encore

Illusion Series Spinoff Novels
Interlude – Jordan's story
Broken Beats – Darren's story
TBA – Eli's story coming fall 2019

http://www.dkellyauthor.com/all-books

www.ingramcontent.com/pod-product-compliance
Lightning Source LLC
Chambersburg PA
CBHW022152240626
47153CB00007B/2622